"I am in your debt. How can I repay you?"

Piper couldn't read Bear's expression with his cowboy hat shadowing his face. "You don't owe me anything. I'll do whatever it takes to protect you and Avery." He rubbed a hand over his jaw. "I've been thinking about things. I want to do what's best for the ranch, so if you're willing to put aside your feelings toward me, then I'll partner with you to get this project up and running."

She studied him a moment. Could she put her feelings aside? At one time, he was her best friend. She admired his quiet strength and the way he valued his family.

She didn't lose just her husband. No, she also lost a friend she'd known since grade school. By her choice. Because being around Bear reminded her of the great times she'd had hanging out at the rodeo with him and Ryland.

Truth was, she missed him.

She nodded. "Yes, I can do that. Let's tell Lynetta we're in."

But debt or no, Piper had a feeling working together might cost more than she could afford.

Heart, home and faith have always been important
to **Lisa Jordan**, so writing stories with those
elements comes naturally. Happily married for
over thirty years to her real-life hero, she and
her husband have two grown sons, and they are
embracing their new season of grandparenting.
Lisa enjoys quality time with her family, reading
good books and being creative with friends.
Learn more about her and her writing by visiting
www.lisajordanbooks.com.

Books by Lisa Jordan

Love Inspired

Stone River Ranch

Visit the Author Profile page at LoveInspired.com.

Redeeming the Cowboy

Lisa Jordan

LOVE INSPIRED
INSPIRATIONAL ROMANCE

LOVE INSPIRED®

INSPIRATIONAL ROMANCE

Recycling programs
for this product may
not exist in your area.

ISBN-13: 978-1-335-59837-0

Redeeming the Cowboy

For questions and comments about the quality of this book, please contact us
at CustomerService@Harlequin.com.

Love Inspired
22 Adelaide St. West, 41st Floor
Toronto, Ontario M5H 4E3, Canada
www.LoveInspired.com

Printed in U.S.A.

The Lord is my strength and my shield;
my heart trusted in him, and I am helped:
therefore my heart greatly rejoiceth;
and with my song will I praise him.
—*Psalms* 28:7

To my mom—you are the strongest person I know. I'm so blessed to be your daughter. You shine your light even on your darkest days. I hope to be like you when I grow up. Love you forever.

Acknowledgments

Lord, may my words glorify You.

My family—Patrick, Scott, Mitchell, Sarah and Bridget. I love you forever.

Thanks to my cousin Rebecca Castilleja for that wonderful conversation as we circled the airport and you shared your career experience for my book research.

Thanks to Jeanne Takenaka for being an incredible craft partner when I was feeling overwhelmed by this story. Thanks to my MBT and JOY Seekers huddles for the prayer support as I wrote this book.

Thanks to Cynthia Ruchti, my awesome agent, and Melissa Endlich, my exceptional editor, for continually encouraging and inspiring me to grow as a writer. So thankful you're on my team. And to the Love Inspired team, who works hard to bring my books to print.

Chapter One

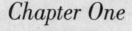

Barrett Stone had spent years on the backs of angry, bucking bulls and managed to stay on for at least eight seconds, so one trail ride wasn't going to kill him.

As the rest of his family rode ahead on the rutted path that cut along the Stone River meandering through South Bend, the original homestead and southern section of the family's Stone River Ranch, Barrett—or Bear to family and friends—hung back, content to allow Ranger, his bay paint horse, to graze alongside the trail.

As the late afternoon early September breeze cooled his sweaty face, Bear removed his cowboy hat and swiped the back of his wrist over his forehead.

Sunlight streaked through a grove of aspens, cottonwoods and pines lining the bank and stretched shadows over Stone River, striping the water black and silver. Ahead of them, the San Juan Mountains turned to copper as the sun settled on their peaks.

Best place on earth. And he had no intention of leaving southwestern Colorado.

The trickling water splashing over rocks beckoned him, and he would've preferred to grab a fly rod and head to the river, but today was reserved for family and enjoying hot dogs and s'mores over the fire.

"Get a move on it, Bear," Macey, his fraternal twin sister, younger by two minutes, called from her horse, Storm, a wedding gift from Cole Crawford, her husband of one month.

He lifted a hand in acknowledgment and nudged Ranger's side with his knee. "Come on, boy. Let's pick up the pace."

The trail cut past his grandparents' homestead, now belonging to Macey and Cole, and opened into a field populated with wildflowers near a small waterfall that fed the river.

Before Macey and Cole's wedding, Bear, Dad and Wyatt, his younger brother, had cleared the area. They rebuilt the crumbling decades-old stone firepit and constructed new picnic tables and matching benches around the fire ring. They'd sectioned off part of the clearing with movable fencing to allow the horses to roam and graze without being tethered.

Growing up, family trail rides had been routine adventures, until his paternal grandparents had been killed in a car accident by a drunk driver ten years ago. Once Macey and Cole returned from their honeymoon, Dad decided it was time to reinstate the monthly rides on Sunday afternoons since it was the one day of the week that they didn't do chores except those necessary for the animals' health and well-being.

While Dad and Cole pitched a tent of kindling to get the fire going, Mom and Everly, Bear's youngest sister, spread out a couple of red-checked tablecloths. Macey and Aunt Lynetta unloaded the food while Bear and Wyatt tended to the horses.

Tanner, his middle sister Mallory's five-year-old son; Mia, Wyatt's two-year-old daughter; and Lexi, Cole's four-year-old daughter, ran in the grass away from the fire, laughing and squealing as seven-year-old Avery Healy, his late best friend's daughter, chased after them.

Once the food had been laid out and the fire was going, Dad called the family together for prayer. As a chorus of amen lifted above the trees, the adults grabbed roasting forks, then perched on the edges of benches while they cooked hot dogs over the flames. With the temps still in the mideighties, the last thing anyone needed was a fire, but no one complained about the heat.

A new tradition. And Bear was all for it.

Just not today. Especially with the letter tucked in his back pocket that he hadn't had the guts to open since receiving it in yesterday's mail. The same one that could redeem or destroy his future.

Bear's eyes drifted across the firepit to Piper Healy, Avery's mother, sitting next to Macey, her new cousin through marriage.

Piper's dark blond hair had been pulled back into a ponytail with a few longer strands of hair curling around her face. Dark sunglasses shielded her eyes, but he knew the color by heart—columbine blue. The same color as the formfitting T-shirt she wore tucked into faded jeans with a frayed hole above the knee that accentuated her long legs. She turned and held his gaze a moment, then returned her attention to Cole, her cousin and Bear's new brother-in-law.

Would things ever return to normal between Bear and Piper?

Not as long as she blamed him for her husband's death. She had every right.

The three of them had been so close—

Bear, Ryland and Piper. Until the day Ryland was thrown from the bull he rode against his best friend's and his wife's wishes.

"Hey, man. What's going on?" Wyatt dropped on the picnic bench next to him and shoved half his hot dog in his mouth.

"Slow down, marine. It's not your last meal."

He grinned around a mouthful of food. "Old habits. Been out of the corps two years, and I'm waiting for my phone to go off, alerting me to a wreck that needs to be investigated. Know what I mean?"

Bear nodded. Oh, yes, he knew all about old habits.

Wyatt nudged his shoulder. "So, does it feel a little weird to have Piper here?"

"Doesn't bother me." He rotated his fork to brown the other side of the meat, keeping his attention on the flames where it belonged.

"Oh, man. You lie. You haven't taken your eyes off her since she and Avery arrived at the ranch with Mace and Cole after church."

Heat having nothing to do with the fire climbed his neck. "A heads-up would've been nice."

Wyatt slapped him on the back. "Why? So you could slink back to your cabin and come up with some excuse why you couldn't join the trail ride?"

He shot his brother a dirty look. "I'm here, aren't I? And I don't slink."

Wyatt jerked his head toward the table. "Only because Mom got a hold of you before you could escape."

"Whatever, dude." Bear dropped his elbows on his knees and focused on the flames racing across the blackened wood. As if his eyes had a mind of their own, they found their way back to Piper, who smiled at something her cousin had said.

His brother let out a laugh that turned everyone's attention to them. Bear ducked his head. "Doesn't your kid need you or something?"

Glancing over his shoulder, Wyatt shook his head. "She's more than happy to sit on Aunt Everly's lap and con her into giving her more marshmallows, so she's good. Which is more than I can say for your dog, man."

Bear jerked the fork out of the fire. Flames licked his hot dog. He swallowed a sigh, pushed to his feet, blew it out and headed to the table. He slid the charred meat into a bun and slathered it with ketchup, mustard and Aunt Lynetta's homemade zucchini relish. Grabbing a napkin and a soda, he returned to the bench next to Wyatt and took a bite.

Dad stood with his back to the river and ran

a hand over his face. Bear tried not to focus on how much silver had crept into his hair over the last months or the deepening of lines in his forehead. His voice still rasped months after healing from the pneumonia-like virus that shut down some of his organs at the beginning of the year and nearly took his life.

He stuffed his hands in his front pockets, and faced the family gathered around the fire. "Hey, guys. Just a little family business that needs to be addressed, then you all can go back to your grub. It's been a tough year. Even though we're blessed to have one another and this land, the ranch is hurting. We need to make some changes. With that in mind, your aunt Lynetta approached your mom and me with an idea, and I'd like you to hear her out." He waved a hand toward his sister. "Take it away, sis."

"Thanks, Deac." Aunt Lynetta moved away from Uncle Pete and took the spot where Dad had been standing seconds ago. Her sunglasses held her dark shoulder-length hair away from her round face.

Wearing jeans and a red T-shirt advertising Netta's Diner, she threaded her fingers together, then looked at everyone. "Family was everything to your grandma. She loved those who carried her name and the friends she gathered close. She was the queen of hospitality who never met a stranger. Last week, I cleared some old boxes of records out of the office at the diner and came across one of Mom's journals. Mom dreamed of having a bed-and-breakfast someday. Being married to a rancher, though, there wasn't enough money to make that happen. Finally, they compromised, and about a year before they died, they decided to build a guest ranch on Stone River property."

"You mean like a dude ranch?" Wyatt stood and tossed another log on the fire, sending up a shower of sparks.

"Call it what you like, but yes."

Bear balanced his elbows on his knees and kept his eyes focused on the ground between his feet as his aunt's words flowed over him.

A guest ranch?

Really, Grandma?

The thought of a bunch of strangers hanging around while he tried to get work done made his skin crawl.

"Where?" Macey asked.

Bear glanced at his sister snuggled next to her husband.

"Out by the lake."

Bear's head shot up. "Lake? The one near my cabin?"

Aunt Lynetta smiled at him, deepening the lines around her warm brown eyes, but he didn't find comfort. "Yes, Bear. Mom and Dad had started their guest ranch on the property adjacent to yours. But nobody's been using that area since they passed away. So now we want to develop it to generate more revenue for the ranch."

"*I* use it daily." The burning in Bear's gut had little to do with the seared hot dog he'd ingested in four bites.

Dad pushed to his feet again and rubbed his hands together. "That's why this affects you most of all. Now that Wallace Crawford has stopped his crusade to buy South Bend for that strip mall, we need to consider different options, especially with last year's drought, cattle prices dropping and feed prices increasing. Otherwise, we *will* be forced to sell off some land, which cuts into your kids' inheritances."

"I get that, Dad, but I don't want a bunch of strangers traipsing through my backyard." Bear grabbed his empty soda can and pitched it in the trash bag next to the table. "Why not put it elsewhere on the ranch?"

"I understand your concern, Bear. I do. About twelve years ago, Mom and Dad had the land surveyed and mapped out for four cabins and a guesthouse." Dad picked up a long stick and stirred the embers. "A well had been dug, utility lines ran, and the area had been cleared, so it makes sense to continue in the same area where they started. When you built your cabin, we hadn't even considered moving forward with their plans."

Bear leaned back and watched the puff of smoke spiral toward the sky.

"After finding Mom's journals and discussing it with your parents, we decided to honor their memories by completing what our parents started. If we start now, we can be ready to open next spring. Bear, we'd like you and—" Aunt Lynetta moved behind Piper and placed her hands on Piper's shoulders "—Piper to oversee the project together."

"Me?" Yanking off her sunglasses, Piper's eyes widened as she twisted and looked up at his aunt in stunned disbelief. "Why?"

"Because with the success of your house-cleaning business, you know how to begin from the ground up. You can take our vision and make it a reality."

Bear threaded his fingers behind his neck and used the heels of his hands to rub away the pain forming at the base of his skull. "When will I have time? The ranch keeps me busy."

His eyes shifted to Piper, who did her very best not to look at him. With her head bent, she ran her thumbs over the arms of her sunglasses.

What was she thinking?

Probably wishing she hadn't come back to the ranch with Cole and Mace.

After that tragic rodeo that claimed her husband's life, Bear was the last person she'd want to work with. Her sob-filled accusation from five years ago echoed inside his head.

You promised you'd watch out for him, Bear! But you didn't talk him out of riding. Now he's gone, and it's all your fault.

For five years, she blamed him. In one horrific afternoon, he lost his two best friends.

Yeah, no…working with Piper would not work. How could he convince his family what a terrible idea this was?

Dad sat on a bench next to Mom, their hands entwined as Mom rested her head on his shoulder.

Bear's gut twisted at the shadows under Mom's eyes that she tried to hide or cover with makeup. Only in their midfifties, his parents were too young to feel old.

Bear's niece, Mia, leaned against him. "You sad, Unca Bear?"

He exhaled, leaned back and pulled her

onto his lap. He tapped the end of her tiny nose. "How could I be sad with a sweet girl like you by my side?"

She curled into him, smelling of baby shampoo, sunshine and campfire smoke. Each of his family members had suffered some sort of loss. Yet they continued to rally around him.

With the year they'd all had so far, he needed to make things easier for everyone, not worse. After all, they were the only ones who believed in him when the media slaughtered him after his fall from grace on live TV.

So, how could he say no? Especially if it was for the good of the ranch? Even if it meant working with the one person who blamed him for destroying her life?

Bear had nothing left to lose.

Why had she agreed to come?

Now Piper was trapped with no way to escape. She couldn't exactly mount her borrowed horse, scoop up her daughter and gallop across the meadow without making some kind of ridiculous scene.

When Macey and Cole invited Piper and Avery to join the Stones' trail ride, Piper came up with several different excuses as to why they couldn't, including she wasn't family. But Cole shot that down, reminding her she was *his* family. And once Avery heard about riding a horse…well, that was it.

What was it with little girls and horses, anyway?

Still, she should've just said no and gone home after church where she wouldn't have had to pretend she wasn't aware of Bear's presence.

Like that was even possible.

Standing over six feet with dark brown hair cut short and combed away from his face and those green eyes that crinkled when he laughed, Bear turned heads wherever he went. With all the work he did on the ranch, the guy certainly didn't need to step foot in a gym.

Not that she noticed or anything.

Truth was, after Ryland died, Piper had excelled in avoiding Barrett Stone with great success. How could she continue their friendship when Bear could've prevented her husband from getting himself killed?

Hanging out with his family, though, put her in much closer proximity than she wanted.

And now Lynetta wanted them to work together? Had the woman bumped her head on the trail? *What* was she thinking?

Lynetta knew how Piper felt about her

nephew, so how could she even imagine pairing the two together would be a good idea?

"You okay?" Macey leaned close, her voice low and filled with concern.

Not trusting her own voice, Piper lifted a shoulder. Her eyes drifted across the fire to Bear sitting on the bench with his young niece curled against his chest.

Dressed in faded jeans and a gray T-shirt, he appeared so comfortable with the little girl wrapped in one arm and her pink elephant tucked under his other.

The look on his face, however, as he listened to his family discuss the guest ranch showed he wasn't too pleased with the conversation.

With the rest of the Stone family waiting for her response, Piper looked at Lynetta. "I don't know, Lynetta. I'm not qualified to get a guest ranch up and running. Today's the first time I've been on a horse in years."

Five years, to be exact.

The woman who was closer to her than Piper's own mother lifted her chin and laughed. "Oh, girl, I disagree. After all, look what you've accomplished in a few short years. You've put yourself through school, graduating with honors, might I add. You run the best housecleaning business in Aspen Ridge.

All while caring for your delightful daughter. And didn't you just tell me you were interested in expanding your business into staging homes for realty companies?"

She shot her a tight smile. "I did. In private."

Lynetta clamped a hand over her mouth. "Oops, sorry, sugar. My bad. There's no one outside this circle I'd trust more to oversee this project. With your business sense and my nephew's brawn, the two of you are the right ones to have this project completed in no time."

If they didn't inflict bodily harm on one another first.

Setting her plate on the bench, Piper stood. She faced Lynetta, crossed her arms over her chest and forced a smile in place. "I appreciate your confidence in me. I really do, but I can't do this."

"Why not?"

Why not?

She should've prepared an answer before she spoke.

"Because…" She searched her brain for the right words to explain her hesitation.

"Because of me." Bear's low tone behind her caused her spine to stiffen.

She turned as he handed a sleeping Mia back

to Wyatt, then pushed to his feet. He shoved a hand in his front pocket. "You're right—Piper is the best person for this job. But she won't do it because you're asking her to partner with me. Ask Wyatt instead, and she'll say yes."

Piper's face flamed, and it had nothing to do with the fire snapping and crackling in front of her. She should protest and say it wasn't true, but she couldn't get her mouth to open in order for the words to come out.

Raising an eyebrow, Lynetta crossed her arms over her chest. "While I love Wyatt like a son, he's not my choice for this project." She turned to Wyatt. "No offense, hon."

Wyatt held up a hand. "None taken."

Lynetta cupped Piper's chin, then turned her away from everyone's watchful eyes. "I wouldn't offer you this project if I didn't think you could do it. I've seen how you've taken on the world for the past nine years. You've got grit and know what it takes to pull yourself up and move forward. But don't say you don't have the skills. I know better."

How was she supposed to answer that?

Other than her daughter, her cousin Cole and now his wife, Macey, Lynetta and her husband, Pete, were the closest ones Piper could even claim as family after her own mother kicked her out of the house at seventeen.

So how could Piper say no to the one woman she owed nearly everything?

Releasing a sigh, Piper ran a hand over her head and combed her fingers through her ponytail. "Can you tell me a little more about the project? Your expectations? A budget? Timeline?"

Apparently pleased by Piper's questions, Lynetta grinned and settled on the bench next to her. "Sure, sweetie. My mother wanted to keep the guest ranch small in order to provide the visitors with personalized experiences tailored to their needs, yet show them a taste of ranching life. Her notes are more than a decade old, so we'll need to update the business plan, recalculate a new budget and hire a crew to construct the cabins and main guesthouse. Pete suggested his nephew Brad's construction company, but we need to see if Brad has room in his schedule for such a large project."

"What's my role in all of this?"

"I'd love for you to review my mother's notes, then help us create a new business plan, for starters. Then maybe you could help us set up the administrative side of the business as well as designing the interior of the cabins, overseeing the landscaping and hiring of staff. I know it's a lot to ask, especially with your business and caring for Avery. But I believe in you and feel you're the right person for this job."

"If she's doing all of that, what are you expecting me to do?" Bear knelt beside his nephew, Tanner, and helped him toast a marshmallow to a golden brown.

Bear always had a way with kids. And the tender, patient way he helped his nephew stirred something inside Piper.

Again, Lynetta grinned, seemingly pleased the discussion was moving in the direction she wanted. "Well, your dad and I thought you could oversee the construction, map out trails for riding, come up with ranch-type activities and maybe find the best spots at the lake for kayaking, fishing and swimming."

Macey moved to the picnic table and reached into the open bag of marshmallows. She slid one on her roasting fork, returned to the bench and handed it to Cole. She jerked her head toward her husband. "If Brad can't, then maybe Cole could talk with his boss and see if they have space in their schedule to get the cabins and guesthouse constructed before winter sets in. I could take photos and set up a website and social media accounts. If we share the different phases of the project, then we can build anticipation for when we open."

Cole pulled a flaming marshmallow out of the fire and blew it out. "We're finishing up some projects right now, but I can talk to Heath, and see what he thinks."

"Once the guest ranch is up and running, I could lead trail rides and help with the water sports." Wyatt shifted his daughter in his arms.

"And I could coordinate family-friendly activities for those with younger children." Everly, Bear's youngest sister, looked up from the picnic table where she sat with Lexi and Avery making beaded bracelets.

Bear lifted his hands, palms out. "Guys, let's slow down, okay? Piper and I haven't even agreed to do this yet. There's a lot to consider before we start delegating responsibilities."

Needing to put a little distance between herself and the enthusiastic Stone family, Piper moved behind the bench and gripped the back. "I agree with Bear."

Bear let out a slow whistle and shook his head. "Somebody make a note on their calendar."

She shot him a dirty look, to which he grinned. Trying to ignore him, she turned her attention back to his family. "I'm not saying yes to this. Yet. Or even at all. I have a lot on my plate right now and can't take on anything that will get in the way of my time with Avery." She glanced at her daughter tying Lexi's bracelet on her tiny wrist. Then she looked at Deacon and Nora Stone and Lynetta and Pete Spencer. "But I'd like to talk more about this when I've had time to do some research and crunch some numbers. You will need to invest a big ole bucket of money to get this guest ranch up and running. You're both business owners, so you know you need to spend money to make money."

Lynetta sat sideways on the bench and tucked her foot under her thigh. She slipped an arm around Piper, pulling her into a side hug, bumping Piper's hip against the seat back. "Girl, you have made my day. Even though it's not the yes I was hoping to hear, I appreciate you at least considering it. How about we get together tomorrow morning and talk things out?"

Still wanting to yell no and escape across the pasture, Piper did a mental scan of her calendar and to-do list for tomorrow, then nodded. She owed Lynetta that much.

Lynetta leaned closer. "If it's money you're worried about, you will be well compensated for your time."

Piper jerked back and shook her head. "No, that thought never crossed my mind."

If she said yes, then she'd be sure Lynetta understood she couldn't take money for doing this project. In fact, it was the one way she could pay Lynetta and Pete back for their generosity over the years when she didn't know how she would've survived being a way-too-young widowed mother forced on her own at too young of an age.

Plus, if she succeeded at making the guest ranch a success, then a referral from the Stone family and Lynetta would go a long way with getting her house-staging side hustle off the ground. And that money could pay the tuition for the private school Everly had been telling Piper about—the one with the gifted program to help Avery get the education she needs.

No, getting paid to take on this project wasn't the issue at all.

She was more concerned with what the project would cost her in the long run if she agreed to work with Bear. How could she protect herself from losing any more to him?

Chapter Two

Get in and get out had been Bear's motto since the media eviscerated his bull-riding career nearly five years ago. Once Mom had learned he was heading into town to meet with Lynetta and Piper, she'd asked him to swing by Blake's Feed & Seed to get chicken feed.

After leaving the sanctuary of the ranch, Bear sat in the truck, waiting for Blake to unlock his store. As soon as it opened, he would get what he needed and get out before anyone had a chance to stop him for a chat. Which usually meant asking when he was returning to the rodeo.

If he'd had his way, he wouldn't have left in the first place.

He glanced at the wrinkled envelope sitting on the console of the farm truck. The same letter he still hadn't opened.

Blowing out a sigh, he reached for it, slid a finger under the sealed flap then pulled out a folded sheet of typed paper. He ran his thumb and forefinger over the creased folds. His stomach rolled as his nerves thrummed.

Just read it, you big chicken.

He unfolded the letter and pressed it against the steering wheel. He scanned the words, then read them a second time. The rodeo association board had accepted his request for a meeting to consider reinstating him.

Cool.

At least they hadn't said no. So there was still a chance. All Bear had to do was keep his nose clean, his head down, and prove to the rodeo board he wasn't the same guy who had lost his temper in front of that reporter on live TV five years ago and was suspended for unsportsmanlike behavior and assault.

Didn't matter that he'd done it to defend someone else's honor. The association hadn't taken that into consideration when he tried to plead his case.

That's because he'd decked Chet McNeil—America's Cowboy—whose father was also the president of the rodeo board, which carried more weight than Bear's chivalry.

Even though he'd been suspended for a year, the desire to head back to the arena lost its appeal without Ryland Healy, his best friend and fellow bull rider. If only Ry would've listened to him instead of climbing into the chute to ride Daredevil…

But now that Everly had let it slip about Avery's opportunity to attend some private school to help with her gifted education, Bear wanted the extra money to help her out. The same way he'd done with Piper. He figured it was the least he could do for his best friend.

As the lights flipped on inside the feed store, a shiny black truck pulled into the parking space next to Bear's. The diesel engine rumbled, competing with the bass thumping from the stereo system. Bear glanced over but couldn't make out the driver through the passenger window. Another cowboy with his hat low and covering his face.

Bear folded the letter and stuffed it back into the envelope. He tossed it onto the passenger seat and reached for the door handle. He had enough time to grab the chicken feed and head to the diner to meet Lynetta and Piper, even though he'd eaten breakfast nearly three hours ago. Then he could return to the ranch where he belonged.

He opened the truck door and swallowed a sigh at the narrow space between the farm truck and the beast next to him hogging more than his share. He closed the door, wincing against the screech of worn metal. He adjusted his cowboy hat, stepped onto the sidewalk and headed for the feed store.

Behind him, another truck door opened. "Well, well, well, if it isn't Slugger Cowboy."

Bear's hand tightened on the door handle as he ground his jaw. Only one person could get under his skin with such a cocky, arrogant voice.

Chet McNeil.

Bear tossed a glance over his shoulder at the conceited jerk. "What do you want, McNeil?"

"Hey, is that any way to greet a friend?" Slamming his door, he grinned, looking even more smug than usual.

Steeling his spine and clenching his teeth, Bear released the door handle to the feed store and faced him. "You're the last person on this planet I'd call a friend."

He ambled toward Bear with his thumbs hooked around the belt loops of his dark wash Levi's like some TV commercial cowboy. His polished hand-tooled leather boots had never seen the inside of a barn. The crisp long-sleeved white shirt with pearl snaps bore the insignia of the rodeo association embroidered above the left pocket. His designer sunglasses shaded his eyes, but they couldn't cover the smirk that twisted his mouth.

McNeil rubbed his jaw and shook his head. "I don't know, Stone. I've had other brawls and I've ended up buying the guy a beer afterward."

"Good thing I don't drink."

"Another one of your many faults, I suppose."

Bear turned away and reached for the door one more time.

"I heard your suspension interview is coming up. I could make or break your career if I wanted." Annoyance laced his voice.

Bear pulled in a deep breath and tried not to let the man's words get under his skin, but sadly, there was an element of truth to them.

Advice his father had given him nearly twenty years ago after his first tangle with Chet when they were ten years old filtered through his head.

Be the bigger man and walk away.

Something Bear should've done five years ago. But what McNeil had said about Piper deserved the fist to the jaw.

He wasn't about to let history repeat itself, though. He'd learned that lesson.

A woman passed between them. Her eyes glued to Chet, she reached for the door handle and grabbed air. Still holding it, Bear opened the door, stepped back and let her pass. He started to follow but a flash out of the corner of his left eye grabbed his attention. Releasing the door, he turned.

Avery Healy, Piper's seven-year-old daughter, with her head bent over the book in her hands, stepped into the street. A car laid on its horn.

Her head jerked up, her eyes widening at the sight of the car coming toward her, and she froze.

"Avery!" Bear roared as he charged after her. He darted between the parked vehicles, grabbed her arm and jerked her to him, pulling her against his chest. He wrapped his arms around her small quivering body and stumbled back onto the sidewalk, his backside slamming against the paved surface.

His heart raced as his breathing quickened. He released his hold and cupped the child's shoulders, turning her attention to him. "Honey, are you okay?"

Eyes wide and filling with tears, she nodded as her bottom lip popped out.

He crushed her against his chest one more time. "Sweetheart, you scared me to death. Where's your mom? I'm surprised you're here by yourself."

A sob shuddering her chest, Avery dashed a hand under her eyes and pointed across the street to his aunt's diner. "She's talking to Miss Lynetta. I forgot my book in the car and asked to get it. She watched me cross the street. I didn't see the car coming. Thank you for saving me."

"Sweetheart, I will always save you." He thumbed away the wetness under her eyes that looked so much like her father's. "How about I walk you back to your mom?"

She nodded and reached for his hand. As they headed for the crosswalk, a deliberate slow clap sounded behind them. "Barrett Stone, rescuer of females of all ages. Way to go, buddy. You haven't lost your touch. Especially with the Healy women."

Curling his free hand into a fist, Bear gritted his teeth.

Be the bigger man and walk away.

Bear had lost his cool twice with the jerk in the past. He wasn't about to do it again, no matter how much he wanted to erase the arrogance off McNeil's face. He wasn't worth Bear's time or energy.

"Avery!"

Bear's head jerked up as Piper raced across the street.

She snatched her daughter away from Bear,

crushed her to her chest and knelt on the sidewalk. She cupped the child's face, then wrapped her arms around her daughter once again. "Avery Renée, you scared the daylights out of me. Remember when I said you needed to stand at the corner and watch for the crosswalk signal to turn?"

Bear swallowed a comment about Piper not following her own words. This wasn't the time nor was it his fight.

Avery nodded. Then she lowered her eyes as her bottom lip puffed out. "I'm sorry, Mom. I forgot."

Piper pressed her cheek against Avery's head. "I'm just glad you're okay, honey."

Avery leaned against Bear's legs and smiled up at him. "He saved me."

"Yes, he did." Piper looked at him, her eyes holding his gaze a moment, then she returned her attention to her daughter. Slowly, she pushed to her feet, her arm still wrapped tightly around Avery's shoulder. She pressed a shaking hand against her mouth, then dropped it to her side. "Thank you. I don't know what we would've done if you hadn't been there."

His parents believed God didn't waste circumstances, good or bad. Despite not wanting to leave the haven of the ranch, maybe

Bear was meant to go to the feed store and be confronted by Chet McNeil just so he could be there to save Avery from getting hit by the car.

"I'll do anything for you and Avery. You know that." He spoke his words low and close to Piper's ear, even though they wouldn't make a bit of difference.

The same promise he'd made to his dying best friend. He may not have been able to save Ryland Healy's life, but he'd spend the rest of his days protecting Piper and Avery. No matter what it took.

Piper hated owing anyone, but now she was in Barrett Stone's debt.

Saving her daughter's life was worth the cost.

Thankfully, Barrett hadn't laid into her about her parenting skills. She had enough critics in her life without needing another.

I'll do anything for you and Avery. You know that.

His promise—the same one spoken five years prior at Ry's funeral—echoed inside her head and sent a shiver down her spine. She closed her eyes against the memory that wanted to shake free and pervade her consciousness.

She didn't need him or anyone else doing anything for her. She was fine on her own. And that was the way it needed to be. Trusting others to be there for her only led to disappointment.

When Avery had begged to grab her book out of the car, Piper reminded her at least three times to wait at the crosswalk and to go when the signal changed. She watched her follow directions crossing the street, but then Piper had taken her eyes off her daughter for only a second. At that moment, Avery walked into the street, her nose in her book, forgetting about the crosswalk rule.

Now she was seated safely next to Piper in a booth with Lynetta's sprinkle pancakes in front of her while she continued reading.

Somehow, Piper needed to get her own heart back to its normal rhythm.

With still-trembling fingers, Piper lifted her half-finished cup of coffee and took a quick swallow. She cleared her throat and tried to focus on Lynetta sitting across from her, arms folded as she waited patiently for Piper to pull herself together.

The woman's dark curly hair had been pulled up in her signature messy bun with a couple of pencils holding it in place. Her brown eyes radiated warmth as she watched

Avery cut into her pancake. A spotless navy-and-yellow apron monogrammed with Netta's Diner stretched over the woman's ample curves.

Piper set her cup back on the saucer, her fingers still trembling slightly. "Okay, where were we?"

"You were asking about my expectations regarding the guest ranch."

"Right. As I mentioned, I won't sacrifice my time with Avery for work. I manage my business in the mornings. I can free up time in the afternoons to work on the guest-ranch project." Piper folded her hands on the table and forced herself to remain composed.

Lynetta covered Piper's fingers with her own, soft and warm. Gentle hands that gave and served unconditionally. "I knew you were the perfect person to take on this project. Like I told you the other night, I realize it's a lot to ask. You have a very busy life."

Piper laughed, then dropped a kiss on Avery's head. "Busy, yes, but it's also boring to some. But I'm okay with that."

Boring kept her daughter safe.

"The last thing Deacon and I want is for you to sacrifice your time with Avery. We value family, and that needs to be guarded. If you're free tomorrow afternoon, we'd love to walk the property with you and Bear to share what we're considering. We'd love any input you two have to offer."

"Bear doesn't seem too excited about partnering with me on this project."

Did she blame him after her accusations from that night? Words she wished she could've taken back, but part of her still believed them to be true.

If Bear had tried harder, then maybe her husband would still be alive and she wouldn't be forced to go through life without him.

"My nephew is a good man who suffered several losses all at once—his best friend, his career and his fiancée. Although I think he's better off without that woman. He holes up at the ranch to protect himself from further hurt. Even though his cabin is across the lake from where we want to develop the guest ranch, I do understand his hesitation."

"I'd forgotten about Staci. She and Bear didn't seem like a good match, but if he loved her..." Her voice trailed off as an image of the curvy barrel racer with wavy blond hair, blue eyes and perfect white teeth came to mind. Neither she nor Ryland had been thrilled when Bear announced their engagement, but if their friend was happy, then they needed to be, too. But once Bear was suspended because he'd hit Chet McNeil, Staci had broken their engagement.

"That girl wanted the fame that came along with Bear winning rodeos. Anyway, getting back to this project, I believe God is calling us to finish what my parents started, and that's what I intend to do. Bear will come around. You'll see."

Piper had her doubts, but she remained quiet. She loved Lynetta's enthusiasm. "I think it's wonderful you want to honor your parents this way."

Lynetta cupped her chin in her hand and stared out the window a moment. "I still can't believe it's been ten years. Some days, it seems like only yesterday Mom was in the kitchen whipping up a batch of her mouth-watering biscuits. And I can still hear Dad's laughter echoing from the grill as he joked with his line cooks."

Piper glanced at Avery, then lowered her gaze to the simple gold band on her left hand. "We don't ever get over that kind of loss, do we?"

"No, sugar, we don't. We learn how to move through it. In time, we smile more and cry less."

The front door opened, bells clanging against the glass. Bear stepped into the diner, paused a moment as he glanced around the room. His eyes landed on her, and he nodded.

She half expected him to hide out at the counter, but he headed toward their booth, his long legs eating up the distance between them.

A shadow fell across their table. Piper shifted her gaze to find her mother-in-law glaring at her. "Sheila, this is a surprise."

Avery jumped up on the bench, nearly spilling her milk, and leaned over Piper. "Hi, Nana."

"Hey, sweetheart. I'm glad to see you're in one piece." Sheila's face softened as she leaned across the table and wrapped Avery in her arms. Then she straightened and returned her attention to Piper. "Seriously, Piper? What were you thinking, letting a girl her age out in the street by herself?"

Piper glanced at Avery, whose eyes widened. She closed her book and tucked her chin to her chest. Piper reached under the table for her daughter's small hand and gave it three gentle squeezes. Their unspoken I love you. Avery smiled and squeezed four times. *I love you, too.*

Piper forced a smile in place. "Sheila, I understand your concern—"

"Concern? If Barrett Stone hadn't grabbed

her, then she would've been hit by that car. I've already lost my only child. I don't care to lose my only grandchild, too." Her voice rose, causing diners to redirect their attention to them.

Forcing herself to remain calm, Piper slid out of the booth and stood. "If you'd like to discuss this more, then let's step outside. I will not have this conversation in front of my daughter."

"Fine." Sheila spun on her heel and yanked the glass door open.

Piper swallowed a sigh. She maintained a civil relationship with Ryland's mother for Avery's sake, but the woman's constant nitpicking about the way she raised her daughter wore on Piper. She glanced at Lynetta. "Would you mind keeping an eye on Avery a moment?"

"Not at all, sugar. You take care of business and I'll enjoy my time with Little Miss."

Smiling her gratitude, Piper pressed a hand to her stomach, then headed for the door, passing Bear, who had hung back at the breakfast counter, observing their sparring.

Just what she needed—another spectator.

Outside, Sheila stood on the sidewalk in front of one of the overflowing window boxes hanging on the front of Netta's Diner.

Her dark hair, highlighted with caramel

streaks, had been cut in an inverted bob. Her manicured nails, flawless makeup and navy tank top tucked into white shorts made Piper feel frumpy in her simple sleeveless sundress covered in a wildflower print and leather sandals.

Piper crossed her arms and rubbed her hands over her chilled skin, despite the warm weather. "Okay, Sheila, let me have it. Tell me what a terrible mother I am and how I should do things differently."

"Don't you take that tone with me." Lines deepened around Sheila's tanned mouth.

Piper shoved her hands in the pockets of her dress. "And don't you lecture me in front of my daughter."

Shaking her head, Sheila settled her over-size sunglasses on her face and sniffed. "If Ryland were alive, he'd be hotter than a hornet's nest about what happened."

"But Ry isn't here. And I'm doing the very best I can to raise our daughter by myself. When Avery asked to get her book, I watched her from this very spot. I reminded her to stop at the crosswalk and wait for the signal to change. Once she got her book out of the car, she lost her focus and stepped into the street in front of the car. Am I happy about it? Of course not. My heart was in my throat.

What a blessing Bear scooped her up. It was an accident. I would *never* allow my daughter to come to harm intentionally, and you know it. Now if there's nothing else, I'd like to return inside. You're welcome to join us, but you must be kind."

Sheila removed her sunglasses and looked at Piper with tear-filled eyes. "I miss him. My boy."

Piper's heart softened and her shoulders slumped. "I do, too."

"May I still have Avery Friday night?" Any displeasure had disappeared from Sheila's face.

"Of course. You know that. She loves Friday nights with her Nana and Pappy."

"Fine. I'll see you then." Without another word, she brushed past Piper and headed down the street.

The diner door opened as Piper pressed her shoulder against the outer wall. She needed a minute before stepping inside and facing the judgmental looks of the customers.

"You okay?"

Piper jumped at the sound of the deep voice behind her, but she didn't need to turn to identify Bear. She nodded, but it was a lie.

She wasn't okay and hadn't been for a very long time.

But she didn't have time to dwell on it. She had a daughter to care for, a business to run and now a new venture to get off the ground so she could give her daughter the life and opportunities she never had.

Hands still in her pockets, Piper faced Barrett. "Sheila saw what happened with Avery and felt the need to discuss my parenting skills. Or lack of them."

He laid a hand on her upper arm, his calloused fingers warm against her skin. "I'm sorry, Piper."

She forced herself not to step away from his touch. He was simply offering comfort. "Certainly not your fault. But I am in your debt. How can I repay you?"

He looked at her a moment, but she couldn't really read his expression with his cowboy hat shadowing his face. "You don't owe me anything. I meant what I said—I'll do whatever it takes to protect you and Avery." He rubbed a hand over his jaw. "I've been thinking about this idea Aunt Lynetta tossed out the other night. I want to do what's best for the ranch, so if you're willing to put aside your feelings toward me, then I'll partner with you to get this project up and running."

She studied him a moment. Could she do that? Put her feelings aside? At one time, he was her best friend. She admired his quiet strength, the way he kept Ryland grounded and the way he valued his family.

She hadn't lost just her husband that day. No, she also lost a friend she'd known since grade school. By her choice. Because being around Bear reminded her of the great times of hanging out at the rodeo with him and Ryland.

Truth was she missed him.

She didn't hate the guy. That emotion was way too strong for what she'd felt these last five years. More like she grieved the double loss.

But maybe it was time to put the past where it belonged and focus on her future.

She pushed away from the wall and nodded. "Yes, I can do that. Let's tell Lynetta we're in."

Even though Barrett said there was no debt, Piper had a feeling working together was going to cost more than she could afford.

Chapter Three

Piper was in over her head, and they hadn't even got started.

But she was too familiar with hard, and she'd see this through, too. Beginning with figuring out Lynetta's map.

How could she have got herself lost only half a mile from the ranch?

She folded her arms over her chest and released a breath. She had cleared her afternoon to accompany Deacon Stone, Bear and Lynetta out to the guest-ranch property.

But when Piper met Lynetta at the diner nearly an hour ago so they could walk the property, Lynetta had been swamped with the lunch rush after one of her servers needed to leave for a family emergency. Not able to get away as planned, Lynetta drew a map quickly on the back of one of the diner's paper place mats and promised Bear and his dad would be there to meet her.

Hopefully that was true, especially since she was half an hour late due to wandering in circles. She looked at the pen-sketched map again and read the directions aloud. "Go through the ranch gate. Instead of pulling into the driveway, turn right. Go past the hoop barn and take a left at the first dirt road. The trail ends in a clearing facing the lake."

Piper had done exactly as Lynetta had said, or so she thought. But there was no clearing. At least not yet. The trail continued much longer than Piper had expected. She'd been walking for the last thirty minutes after parking her car on the side of the road. The trail Lynetta mentioned hadn't looked wide enough to move her SUV through without inflicting some sort of damage to the paint. A risk she couldn't afford to take.

She slapped another mosquito and dragged the back of her hand across her sweaty forehead. Her skin felt as dry and thirsty as her throat. She'd be a lovely shade of pink later tonight.

Maybe she needed to head back to her car and swing by the ranch house. Nora, Bear's mom, could point her in the right direction.

Or she could give Cole a call. If he didn't know, he'd put her in touch with Macey.

As she pulled her phone out of her tote bag holding her empty water bottle and tablet, a dog barked somewhere in the distance. Piper paused, cocked her head and listened.

The dog barked again, this time coming from the right. Piper pivoted and retraced her steps in that direction. A narrow path cut through the trees and opened to a freshly mowed yard wedged between the lakeshore and a gorgeous wood-sided cabin capped with an evergreen metal roof and matching shutters.

A black-and-white dog barked and raced across the yard toward her. She stiffened and braced for impact. But a sharp whistle sounded, and the dog stopped, then sat on its haunches, panting.

Something about the animal seemed familiar.

Piper shoved her sunglasses on the top of her head and searched for whomever had given the command.

A man wearing a T-shirt and cargo shorts rounded the corner of the house. He whipped something into the lake, then called, "Dakota, fetch."

The dog rocketed after the object.

Dakota?

Her late husband's black-and-white English shepherd puppy had been named Dakota...

The man crossed the deck in front of the cabin and made his way to where she remained rooted in his yard.

Bear.

She groaned. This must be his place.

"Piper. What are you doing here?" Bear's navy T-shirt stretched across his muscled chest as he dragged a hand through his hair and settled a dusty Broncos ball cap back on his head.

She lifted a shoulder, then pulled out the crinkled map. "I went to the diner, but your aunt couldn't get away as planned, so she drew me a map. I guess I got lost. I heard the dog bark and thought maybe someone could point me in the right direction."

"Let me see that." He moved behind her and leaned over her shoulder, standing so close she could feel the heat from his skin. He smelled faintly of horse, hay and sunshine. She debated between breathing deeply or taking a step away from him.

He chuckled softly, the sound sending a mild shiver down her spine. He jabbed the map. "Here's the problem. Aunt Lynetta forgot that the trail forks. You should have taken a left, and that would have put you where you needed to be. A right brought you to my place."

"She was really busy when she drew it." Her head jerked up, nearly cuffing him in the chin. "So this is the place you mentioned the other night."

"Bought the land from Dad and Lynetta and built the cabin with rodeo money."

"It's gorgeous. And a bit secluded."

A shadow flickered across his leaf green eyes. "Yeah, that's the point."

The dog charged out of the water and shook himself on the shore before bounding across the grass. He dropped a dripping yellow tennis ball at Bear's bare feet.

Picking it up, Bear scratched the dog's muzzle. "Good boy, Kota." He threw it again. "Fetch it back."

The dog flew after the ball, splashing into the water, and paddled to where the ball floated on the surface.

Piper shaded her eyes with her hand as she watched the dog retrieve the ball once again. "Ryland had a puppy named Dakota."

Bear shifted, pocketing his hands. Lines deepened around his eyes as he squinted against the sunshine reflecting off the lake. "When you returned Dakota to Ry's parents after his death, they weren't in the right place to handle a puppy. But they didn't want to surrender him to the shelter, so they asked if I wanted him."

"I didn't realize." Piper blinked away an echo of a memory that slipped past the barricade she'd erected so long ago. She pulled her phone out of her bag and checked the time. "Since I missed our appointment, let's reschedule another time to check out the property."

"No need. We're both here now, so I'll call Dad. He can meet us. There's a Gator parked out back. We'll drive to the property." He whistled for Dakota, who seemed content to paddle in the water. The dog swam to shore, shook his fur and raced after Bear.

Piper followed them and climbed in the passenger side of the mud-splattered utility vehicle while Dakota jumped in the back. Bear stowed his phone in his pocket, hopped into the driver's seat and started the engine. They cut through a different path than the one Piper had taken and stopped in the middle of a field that looked more like what Lynetta had described.

Crossing his arms on the steering wheel, Bear looked at her. "Dad'll be a minute. You want to wait in the shade or take the five-cent tour?"

"Tour sounds good." She stepped out of the Gator, pocketed her phone and left her tote bag on the seat.

They parked and walked back to an area that faced the small lake. A slight breeze rippled the surface.

Maybe she should've worn something a little more presentable than a yellow The Clean Bee T-shirt and denim shorts. Or even a hat to keep the sun off her face. At least the ponytail kept her neck a little cooler.

He pointed to her shirt. "I hear your business is going well."

She glanced down at the bee holding a dusting cloth logo and nodded. "I just hired another cleaner to join our team."

"What's this staging business Aunt Lynetta mentioned?"

"One of my clients works in real estate and asked me to do some staging in his homes. Before he does open houses, I go into the homes or apartments, clean them, then prep them for showing by adding homey touches such as throw pillows, knitted blankets, candles, flowers, plates of fresh-baked cookies. He's passed my name on to his colleagues. So now I'm developing a little side hustle, which is good because I'll have tuition to pay in January. Not to mention house hunting."

"Going back to school?"

"No, Avery's in the gifted program at Aspen Ridge Elementary. While it's a wonderful school, the program is a little limited. Everly, who happens to be Avery's teacher, was telling me about a private school in Durango with an excellent gifted education program. I want to give my daughter the very best I can afford, so I'm planning to enroll her and find a place for us to live in Durango."

"So you're leaving Aspen Ridge."

He spoke so quietly that Piper wasn't sure if he was commenting to her or himself.

"Well, let's get started then." Giving her a tight smile, he waved a hand toward the overgrown property fringed with grass and wildflowers and separated by rows of trees. "Like Aunt Lynetta said, my grandparents planned to have four guest cabins along with a large guesthouse that would have a community dining room, kitchen, office, rec room and a gathering room."

"From what I saw yesterday, they had most of the details figured out."

"Pretty much. My grandma loved to be around people."

"I remember. I loved working for her at the diner."

"That's right. I'd forgotten you worked there."

"She and Lynetta treated me like family." Piper snapped a few pictures with her cell phone as she walked around one of the sections nestled in its own pine grove. Then she crossed the grass to where the water lapped at the stony shore.

Slipping off her sandals, Piper dipped her toes in the lake and allowed the cool water to run over her hot feet. Too bad she couldn't plunge in like Dakota had done.

Hearing the closing of a vehicle door and Dakota's bark, Piper slipped her feet back in her sandals and made her way back as Deacon Stone joined Bear.

Bear's father tilted back his cowboy hat, revealing a tanned face weathered by years of being outdoors, and held out a hand. "Hey, Piper. Good to see you again."

She placed her hand in his calloused fingers. "Thanks, Mr. Stone. Same here."

"Call me Deacon, young lady. Mr. Stone was my father." He settled an arm around her shoulders and steered her back to the field. "I hear Bear started the tour without me."

"My fault for being late. I don't want to take up any more of your time than necessary."

"Nonsense. You're here to help us. We're the ones who need to be more cognizant of your time. So, what do you think?"

She waved a hand over the property. "The area's gorgeous. With it being away from the ranch house, your family will have plenty of privacy. I'm not sure how much you want to develop this section, but the view of the lake is gorgeous, especially with the mountains in the background. I'd suggest building the cabins to face the water. Maybe clear away some of the trees by the shore and include a gazebo or maybe a pavilion with tables and a dock with built-in benches or chairs at the end. As for the cabin interiors, I'm thinking a Western theme, of course, but with casual elegance."

Deacon rubbed a hand over his chin. "A little class. I like it. Sounds like you've been thinking about this."

"Well, I had some initial thoughts based on my conversation with Lynetta yesterday. Now that I can see the property, I have a better understanding of what we're working with. I've taken some pictures. I'll do more research and present my ideas to you guys before we proceed with hiring a construction crew." An alarm sounded on her phone. She dug it out of her back pocket and silenced it. "I'm so sorry, but I have to pick up my daughter from school."

Deacon waved away her apology. "No worries. Maybe you and Bear can meet later tonight to discuss more of the details."

Her eyes volleyed between Deacon, who raised an eyebrow, and Bear, whose jaw tightened.

She ran a thumb around the case of her phone and glanced at Bear. "Um, yeah, sure. If Bear wants to, that is."

He lifted a shoulder. "Might as well get moving on it."

"Avery has dance after school, then we'll eat dinner. I'll help her with homework, then it's time for bed. How about seven thirty or eight? That will give me some time to put some thoughts together."

"Sure, works for me."

She wasn't sure if she was ready to spend an evening with him, but they'd committed to working together and needed to move forward with the project. She'd get through it because this wasn't about her but what was best for her daughter.

This partnership with Piper wasn't going to work.

Bear had agreed to meet at her house, but

he hadn't realized he'd be working with someone who had control issues.

Together less than half an hour and he'd had to temper his tone twice already. Knowing Avery was home and tucked into bed forced him to keep his voice low. He learned pretty quickly that Piper liked doing things her way. Maybe that's why she ran her own company—she didn't want to answer to someone else.

He skimmed the website she'd pulled up on her laptop, trying not to let the price tag of some of the furnishings on the page cause his heart to stop. "Piper, all I'm saying is Stone River is a working ranch, not a wealthy vacation spot. You know my family—we're pretty down-to-earth. I want anyone to be able to come and get a taste of Western life without breaking the bank to go on vacation."

She laughed, a sound that tripped his pulse. "No, you don't. If you had your way, this guest ranch wouldn't be happening, and you could stay in your secluded house, living out your days as a hermit."

Hermit reminded him of a grizzled old geezer with a long gray beard, suspenders and a cranky attitude. Was that how she saw him? Was that why she stayed away after Ry was killed?

She'd changed into a soft green T-shirt and tan shorts. Her hair had been taken out of its earlier ponytail and fell over her shoulders in waves. The early evening sunlight caught it and turned it to gold. He longed to touch it, to twirl it around his fingers, to see if it felt as silky as it looked. Her nose and cheeks turned pink from her afternoon on his family's property.

Even without makeup and dressed in casual clothes, she was the prettiest woman he'd ever seen. Maybe that was why he'd fallen head over heels in love with her in junior high. But instead of moving forward on his emotions, he'd taken a very painful step back when his best friend voiced his interest.

But what if he'd spoken up first?

No sense in dealing in what-ifs. He'd lost out, and he'd been placed firmly in the friend zone. Or in Piper's opinion, maybe the frenemy zone.

"Listen, Bear, I don't have a degree in interior design, but I can work with a budget." Her voice pulled him back to the conversation at hand. "I have an eye for detail and can still create a stylish setting with an economical price tag. I've had years of practice at stretching a dollar. You don't want the guest ranch to appear cheap, nor do you want to give the

experience away. You want a solid ROI—
return on your investment. Otherwise, the
ranch will be losing money instead of turning a profit. Besides, I'm not actually buying
products from that site. I simply like the style
and felt it would be fitting for the cabins."

"You're right." Bear swallowed a growl and
scrubbed his hands over his face. "Change
needs to happen, and somehow, I'll learn to
roll with it."

Grinning, Piper reached across the table
scattered with notes for her cell phone, tapped
an app and a microphone appeared on the
screen. "Mind repeating that? The you're-
right part, I mean?"

"Funny girl." He grinned, hoping it eased
some of the tension between them.

She shot him a smile that struck him in
the chest. "Yes, I'm a real comedian. Seriously, though. I know how hard change can
be. I've been doing plenty of it since Ryland
died." Reaching for her glass of iced tea, she
drained it and stood. "Need a refill?"

"No, thanks," Bear said. He drained his
glass and followed her into the small yet
immaculate kitchen. The silver appliances
gleamed. Not a crumb lingered on the granite
countertop. No dishes in the sink. Not even
the gray cabinets had a scuff. If it hadn't been

for the plants lining the windowsill or the dish towel hanging next to the sink, he would have wondered if anyone even used the room.

Same with the rest of the house.

When she invited him in, he had entered a living room that looked like something from a design magazine. A navy-and-white-striped couch and matching chair sat in front of a corner stone fireplace with pictures of Ryland, Piper and Avery lining the wooden mantel.

Not a single picture of Ryland at the rodeo, though. Nor any of the numerous trophies he'd won riding bulls.

Bear handed her the empty glass and leaned against the counter. "Speaking of change, listening to Aunt Lynetta list all of your achievements the other night was pretty impressive. I hadn't realized your business was doing so well."

She lifted a shoulder, then opened the dishwasher and set both glasses on the top rack. After she closed it, she washed her hands, then wiped out the sink so no water droplets remained. "Well, we really haven't been on speaking terms."

He raised an eyebrow. "I'm not the one who stayed away. I offered my help, but you shut me out."

Folding her arms over her chest, she lifted

her chin. "What'd you expect, Bear? You could've talked Ryland off that bull, but you let him ride anyway, knowing he wasn't at his best mentally or physically."

Bear clenched his jaw. "Not this again. He was a grown man who made his own choices. And for the hundredth time, I did try to talk him out of it, but he refused to listen. I've been trying to tell you that for years, but you won't believe me. It's the same ole song, but I'm done dancing."

Too many falls had created head trauma that spiraled his best friend into a sea of depression. Bear should've forced Ryland not to ride, especially after the first round that day had jarred his brain. But Ryland had protested—he was fine and needed the points to retain his rodeo association membership. The bull had given him a final toss, and Bear carried the guilt since the moment his friend's lifeless body hit the arena ground.

Bear looked out the kitchen window. Dusk settled over the ranching community. Streaks of orange and gold colored the sky. No wonder he was tired.

He rubbed a forefinger and thumb over his burning eyes. "Listen, I need to be up at four, so let's call it a night. I'll see what I can do about freeing up time tomorrow to get together and continue the planning."

The light had dimmed in Piper's blue eyes. Any time Ryland was mentioned, the tension between them increased. He didn't like being the cause of her pain. He longed to draw her into his arms, but that would do nothing more than cause more friction between them.

Piper held out her hand. "Give me your phone."

"Why?"

"So I can put my contact information in it. You can't call or text if you don't have my number."

"Right." He pulled it out of his back pocket and handed it to her.

Her thumbs danced across the keypad, then she returned it to him. She walked him back to the living room. As he shoved his feet in his shoes, a quiet knock sounded on the door.

"Excuse me." Piper brushed past him and opened it, wreathing him in the floral scent she favored. She spoke through the screen door. "Eugene, hey. What brings you by this evening?"

Over her shoulder, he saw a man with graying curly hair leaning heavily on a cane with a wrapped plate in his other hand. "So sorry to drop by so late, but my sister Jess and her husband, Rod, had come to dinner. They just left, but she brought me some cupcakes. I can't eat them all, and I thought you and little Avery would enjoy some."

"That's so sweet." She opened the door and stepped back. "Please come in."

Eugene squinted through rimless glasses. "Is that Barrett Stone I see standing there?"

"Yes, it is."

"Well, I'll be." Eugene stepped inside Piper's apartment, and she closed the door behind him. "I used to follow your and Ryland's rodeo careers. You have a gift with those animals, young man."

Bear nodded. "Thank you, sir."

Piper glanced between the two men. "Bear, this is Eugene Shaw, my landlord and good friend. In fact, he was one of my first clients."

Bear thrust a hand at the older man. "Nice to meet you, sir."

Eugene shook his hand and smiled at Bear. "This one's got manners. He's a keeper."

Piper's cheeks reddened as she laughed off Eugene's remark. "Bear and I aren't dating, Eugene. We're working on a project for his family."

"If you say so, dear." He handed the cupcakes to Piper. "No rush in getting the plate back to me. I know where to find you."

Her eyes softened as she smiled at Eugene. "You're a sweet man. Avery will love these." Piper looked at Bear. "Eugene has a small farm outside of town, and he's an award-winning apiarist. In fact, he runs a beekeeping program that helps veterans with PTSD. I named my business after him…sort of."

Bear turned to Eugene. "Seriously? That's cool. Could a program like that be geared for cowboys recuperating from rodeo trauma?"

Leaning on his cane, Eugene scratched his chin. "I don't see why not. You interested in starting something like that?"

Bear lifted a shoulder. "Quite honestly, I'd never considered beekeeping, but I've thought about looking into some sort of program to help cowboys struggling with the aftereffects of rodeo injuries. Problem is, the lack of time and resources."

Eugene clapped him on the shoulder. "Let's get together and talk. I can't help with time, but I do have some connections for resources."

At the mention of the rodeo, Piper's eyes dimmed once again. Perfect time for him to leave before they had another discussion about his failures as a friend.

"Thanks. I appreciate it. Maybe after we finish my family's project. I'll have my hands full until then." He lifted a hand. "Piper, I'll contact you tomorrow."

Eugene steered toward the door. "I need to be going, too. Give Avery a hug from me."

"Will do. Have a good night, guys." She closed the door behind them.

Eugene had parked a compact car behind Bear's Jeep. "I'll get out of your way quick enough."

"No rush. Nice to meet you, sir. I'd really like to sit down with you sometime to learn more about your program."

Eugene cupped the top of his cane with both hands and leaned forward. "I'd like that, too. Pardon an old man's nosiness, but I worry about Piper. She's a good one. Takes such great care of that little one and works hard, too. Just be careful. Her heart's fragile, you know."

Bear pulled keys out of his pocket. "Yes, sir. I promise not to do anything purposefully to hurt her. Or Avery. Ryland was like a brother, so they're like family to me."

"Glad to hear it." Eugene clapped him on the shoulder, then made his way to his car.

He'd do his part to get the guest ranch going in order to honor his grandparents' memory. Even if that meant biting his tongue over her control issues in order for their partnership to work out.

Now that she was back in his life, he didn't want to drive her away again. The last thing he wanted was to hurt anyone he cared about, including Piper. Even if she kept him at arm's length to protect herself.

Chapter Four

After Ryland's final toss from Daredevil, the bull that stole his life, Bear had no problem learning to say no when others asked more of him than he could give.

Except when it came to Victor Flynn, one of his mentors in the rodeo arena.

When Victor called that morning with the news that his daughter had gone into premature labor and needed help caring for her twin toddlers, Bear assured him very quickly that yes, he would take over Victor's Lil Riders group while his friend and his wife ventured out of town. And, of course, it wouldn't be a problem moving it to the arena at Stone River.

Even better for him, actually.

He stared at the gangly group of five-to eight-year-olds wearing toothy grins and oversize cowboy hats. Had he made a mistake in saying yes?

Sure, he knew a thing or two about rodeo, but not much about little kids. Well, except for his nephew, Tanner, who joined the fray.

At least he didn't have to go in alone.

Gavin Copeland, the best mechanic in Aspen Ridge and Victor's right hand, showed up to assist Bear with keeping the little riders on top of the sheep.

Louisiana born and bred, and built like a fence post, Gavin had headed west to marry the girl of his dreams and then spent thirty years building their lives together until she passed away last year. Now Gavin filled his time helping anyone who needed a hand.

Bear would do his best, and that was all Victor expected from anyone. If his mentor could do it while pushing sixty, then Bear could handle a few kids for an hour on a Saturday.

Pushing away from the fence that ringed the arena, Bear rubbed his hands together and scanned the motley group. Boys and girls with dirt on their cheeks and hope in their eyes stared back at him.

He tipped up his hat and crouched in front of them, wincing as his knee popped. He rested his forearms on his thighs. "My name's Barrett Stone, but you can call me Bear. Victor is a good friend of mine. He had a family emergency, so I'm stepping in until he comes back."

Bear pointed to a boy wearing worn Levi's with blown-out knees, a plaid pearl-snap shirt and an oversize cowboy hat. "What's your name, little man?"

"Liam McNeil."

McNeil? Seriously?

Bear swallowed a sigh and forced a smile as he stuck out his hand. "Nice to meet you, Liam."

The kid eyed him. "My uncle Chet said you were kicked out of the rodeo. Is that true?"

Man, nothing like pulling punches on the first day.

Bear looked at the kid and nodded. "I let my anger get the best of me, and I hit someone. That was the wrong decision to make." He glanced at Gavin. "But we're going to help you to learn how to make better choices, so you'll do well from the beginning. How's that sound?"

Liam nodded and tipped up the brim of his hat.

The rest of the kids rattled off their names, but no one asked any other questions.

Eyeing Gavin, Bear stood, then jerked his head toward the group. "I'm sure you know all about them. Best way to start?"

Still clad in his navy grease-stained overalls from the garage, Gavin removed his grubby ball cap and scratched the top of his balding head. "Just do your thang, Bear. These kids are good 'uns and just wanna learn."

Bear nodded as his eyes skimmed the arena. "Okay, riders, we're going to work on mutton bustin'. You know what that is, right?"

Most of the kids nodded and squinted against the morning sun casting warm rays over them.

Liam lifted his arms, then dropped them at his sides. "We know how to do that already."

"Yeah? I'm sure you do. But it's always good to keep on learning. Who wants to be my first volunteer?"

They looked at each other and tried to shrink into their shadows.

"What about you, Liam?"

The kid's eyes widened as he glanced at his friends, then jerked a thumb toward his chest. "Me?"

"Sure. You're strong and smart. Let's show your friends what a real sheep rider looks like."

With all kinds of doubt lining his face, Liam looked at the others one more time, then dropped his gaze to his feet and shook his head. "I don't think so."

Bear crouched in front of him. He rested a hand on the kid's bony shoulder. "Hey, man. I get it. You don't know what's gonna happen. You don't wanna fall and get hurt. And you certainly don't want your friends to laugh at you. Am I right?"

Liam nodded.

"Mr. Copeland and I are here with you every step of the way, okay?"

Liam eyed him again, then nodded. "Okay."

Bear grinned and gave his shoulder a gentle squeeze. "Great. Let's gear up. Our number one goal is to keep you safe. And we want to keep the animals safe, too. Even though we're not using a real sheep today, it's always good to keep those two rules in mind. Got it?"

They nodded. Gavin dropped the gear bag next to Bear. He dug through the canvas bag and pulled out a helmet and a padded protective vest. He held the vest while Liam slid it on, then Bear secured it in place. He removed Liam's hat, then placed the helmet on the kid's head, tightening the strap, and tapped it gently on the side. "How's that feel, buddy?"

Liam gripped the vest and then adjusted the helmet on his head. "Fine."

"Good." Bear pushed to his feet and passed Liam's hat to Gavin. "Let's review how to hold on to the sheep. You don't have a saddle, so how do you hang on tight?"

Tanner, Bear's five-year-old nephew, waved his hand in the air. "You have to use your knees and legs."

Bear grinned. "Great job, Tanner. You hold on to the sheep's wool and grip the animal with your knees and legs." Walking backward toward the fence, he stopped next to a wagon Gavin had brought along with the gear bag. Bear picked up the dusty, scratched black handle. "I'm going to use this wagon and show you how to hold on tight."

Bear pulled Victor's training wagon filled with hay, pillows, and wrapped in faux sheepskin in front of the row of riders. "Liam, now remember—you need to climb on this pretend sheep and lay on your belly. Use your knees and legs to hold on to its sides. Your goal is to hold on tight for eight seconds, okay?"

Liam scrambled onto the makeshift sheep and gripped both sides of the covered wagon.

"Ready?"

Liam nodded and gave Bear a thumbs-up.

Bear lifted his chin toward Gavin, who held up a stopwatch.

"Okay, buddy. Hold on tight." Bear grabbed the handle and started running. He glanced over his shoulder. Liam grinned as they bumped over the dirt arena.

Bear ran back and forth and jostled Liam as much as he could to give the little guy a feel of riding a stampeding animal.

Gavin blew the whistle around his neck. "Time!"

With his heart pounding and muscles thrumming, Bear dropped the handle and thrust both fists in the air. "Woo-hoo! You did it, Liam. Great job!"

Liam scrambled off the wagon and slapped a small hand against Bear's palm. Then he jerked his closed fist to himself. "Yes. I did it." He sauntered back to his friends, chin a little higher and back a little straighter.

Bear removed his hat and swiped sweat off his brow with the back of his arm. Then he settled his hat in place.

As his gaze swept the yard, he caught sight of a silver SUV parked in front of the ranch house. And someone leaned against it, watching them.

His eyes narrowed.

Not a parent. At least not one who had dropped off one of the kids attending the morning session.

Piper.

His heart slammed against his chest. He

hadn't expected her to show up at the ranch without notice, but he wasn't complaining. Any excuse to see her again.

How'd he miss hearing her pull up?

He lifted a hand, then turned to Gavin. "Mind taking over a minute?"

"Not at all." The older man grinned as Piper moved from the car and walked over to the arena, carrying a cardboard cylinder. Then he touched the brim of his hat. "Mornin', Piper."

"Hey, Gavin. Good to see you."

"You, too, Sunshine. Thanks for knocking the dust off the ole house yesterday. Looks great as always. Appreciate it. How's Avery doing?"

"You're welcome. I love your home. She's doing very well. Thanks for asking."

"Give her my love." He touched the brim of his hat, then ambled to the group of kids.

"Will do. Thanks." She watched him a moment, then turned back to Bear, the smile sliding from her face.

"Hey, Piper. What's going on?" He took in her familiar-looking yellow The Clean Bee shirt and cuffed black shorts. She wore a pair of black flip-flops and had her hair gathered in a messy bun.

She lifted the cylinder. "The plans arrived

from the architect, so I stopped by to see if we could set up a time to review them."

"That was fast. Less than a week. I figured it would take a couple, at least."

She lifted a shoulder. "I called in a favor."

He raised an eyebrow. "What works for you?"

She thumbed through the calendar app on her phone. "Is this evening too soon?"

Bear did a mental review of his schedule. Once the kids left, he'd be haying with Dad and Wyatt. "I should be free."

"How about around seven? I promised Avery a picnic at Eugene's after she returned from her grandparents'. We could meet back at my place afterward."

He rested an elbow on the fence rung. "I'll be there."

Shielding her eyes with her hand, Piper nodded toward the kids still huddled around Gavin, Liam and the makeshift wagon sheep. "Aren't those the kids from Victor's rodeo camp?"

He glanced at them, then looked back at her. "Yes. I'm a little surprised you'd know that."

"Victor and his wife are clients. I've been to their ranch when he's been working with them."

"He was called out of town and asked me to take over."

"His wife called me, too, and canceled their cleaning appointment for next week. Said she wasn't sure when they'd be back. I didn't realize you were taking over. Not that I need to know or anything. Definitely none of my business." She cast her eyes to the ground.

He wouldn't mind making it her business, but he stayed quiet as he studied the way the sun shone on her head, creating a crown of gold. With her head barely reaching his shoulder, it wouldn't take anything to wrap her in his arms.

She looked up at him, something he couldn't quite decipher shifting in her eyes. "You're good with them, Bear. Patient. And kind. They need those words of encouragement."

Her quiet tone absent of any sarcasm or censure sent a shot of warmth to his gut. He was surprised she'd noticed. But maybe she'd see he wasn't the evil one she'd seemingly built up in her head through the years.

He scrubbed a hand over his jaw, trying not to let her words open a sliver of hope in his chest. "You're welcome to bring Avery by and let her do a little mutton bustin'. I'm sure she knows all the kids."

Her eyes darkened. "You can't be serious."

He lifted a shoulder. "Sure, why not?"

"I've told you already—I refuse to allow my daughter to have anything to do with the rodeo. It's taken enough from us already, and I'm not about to risk Avery's life, too."

He shook his head and gripped the fence rung that created a barrier between them. "Come on, Piper. Riding a sheep is nothing like riding a bronc or a bull. You know that."

Her eyes narrowed as she fisted a hand on her hip. "Tell me, Bear, how did you get started with the rodeo?"

He jerked his head toward the boys, feeling his neck warm under her stare. "Doing what they're doing—mutton bustin', then moved up to calves and then horses."

"Exactly. By giving Avery a taste, then she's going to want more. And I can't allow that."

"Even if it's for her own good?"

"How do you know what's for her own good?"

"She has her father's blood in her veins."

"And she's growing up without that father, thanks to the choices he made, remember? She needs to stay as far away from the rodeo and anyone associated with it as possible."

Anyone associated? Was she saying he was off-limits, too?

While Bear wanted to argue about Piper being irrational, he swallowed his words. Now was not the time nor the place. Besides, she wasn't in the right frame of mind to listen to him, anyway. As far as Piper was concerned, there was only black and white when it came to the rodeo. No shades of gray.

And apparently that included him.

If it weren't for her involvement in his family's project, he was sure she'd continue to avoid him.

He wanted on the back of a bull more than anything, but if he had to choose between reclaiming his career and the woman who stole his heart so many years ago, he couldn't say honestly what choice he'd make.

If Piper gave a hint of interest toward him, then he'd give up his dream in a heartbeat. But she'd made it clear more than once there could never be anything between them. So he'd focus on the other dream and continue to live without her.

Stopping by Bear's rodeo camp had been a huge mistake.

The moment she'd stepped out of her car and listened to the way he'd coaxed Liam McNeil onto that silly fake sheep, her heart nearly melted.

The man had a way with kids. He was a natural encourager.

No wonder Ryland had always looked up to him.

In a different environment, he'd be the kind of guy she'd want in her life. And in Avery's.

But with his strong desire to return to the rodeo, she couldn't lose her heart to another bull rider. No matter how charming he may be. She needed to focus her attention on his family's project and keep him at arm's length where it was safer for all of them.

Her doorbell rang, and her pulse raced. She blew out an exasperated breath and headed for the door.

Knock it off.

At least she didn't have to worry about him showing up tonight.

Maybe she had chickened out and canceled their meeting by text. She just needed... What? More excuses to keep him at a distance? There was a reason she stayed away from Bear Stone. The man could get under her skin quicker than anyone. That smile. The way his eyes crinkled when he laughed.

Even when he showed up at her apartment for the first time to discuss the guest-ranch plans, her rooms seemed to shrink around him. He had a presence that made her feel things she hadn't allowed herself to feel in a very long time.

The man was dangerous, and she needed to keep her distance.

"I got it, Mom." Scooting off the couch, Avery raced for the door, her braids bouncing behind her. She pulled it open. "Hi, Uncle Bear. Are you going on our picnic, too?"

Piper swallowed a groan, not only at the new nickname Avery had taken to giving Bear but also at his presence.

"Hey, Bookworm." He tapped the tip of her nose. "No. I just stopped by to check on you and your mom."

"Moooom. Uncle Bear's here."

"I'm right behind you, Ave. No need to yell." Reaching over Avery's head, she opened the door wider. "Hey, Bear. You didn't get my text?"

"Mom, can Uncle Bear go on our picnic, too?" Avery bounced on the balls of her feet.

"I'm sure he's too busy to join us, Avery."

"Actually, I'm free the rest of the evening, remember?" Raising an eyebrow, Bear leaned a shoulder against the door frame. "I got it. Like I told Avery, I wanted to swing by and make sure everything was okay."

Okay?

Hardly.

She folded her arms over her chest, not moving away from the door to allow him inside. "Tonight's not a good night to review the plans, after all."

"So you said." He waved his phone at her. Then his face creased into concern. "What's going on?"

With Avery watching her and Bear's gaze causing the hairs on her arms to stand, her flimsy excuses melted. Releasing a sigh, she dropped her hands to her sides and stepped back. "Come in. I guess we have a few minutes to look them over."

Avery jerked on her arm. "What about our picnic, Mom?"

Piper cupped Avery's chin. "This won't take long, honey. Then we'll go."

Avery clapped her hands. "I have a better idea—Uncle Bear can join us." She turned to him. "You said you were free, right?"

"I did." He grinned at her daughter, then slid his gaze over to Piper. "But I don't want to impose."

"Impose? What does that mean?"

He dropped to his haunches and clasped his hands. "It means I don't want to get in the way of any plans your mom's made already."

Avery launched herself into Bear's arms. "She won't care. Right, Mom?"

What could she say without sounding like a jerk? No, Bear couldn't go because his presence unraveled her?

The scent of his soap drifted toward her. His damp hair darkened from a recent shower. Dressed in a gray T-shirt advertising Wylie's Western Wear, jeans and his worn boots, he looked like he'd stepped out of the pages of a catalog.

She shot them a tight smile. "Not at all, honey."

Bear's lips curved at the lie, but he didn't say anything.

Turning away from him, she eyed the basket on the dining room table she'd packed with pitiful chicken salad sandwiches, grapes and chocolate chip cookies. Certainly nothing substantial for a man of his size.

"Well, you're welcome to join us, if you'd like."

Please say no.

"Sure, sounds great." He straightened and shoved a hand in his front pocket, his other holding on to Avery's.

Piper waved a hand at the cardboard cylinder resting on the dining room table. "Fine. Look over the plans while I finish getting our picnic together."

"How about we look them over while we eat? Where is this picnic, by the way?"

Before Piper could answer, Avery pulled on his arm and jumped up and down. "We're going to Uncle Eugene's farm. He has a surprise for me, so Mom promised we'd have a picnic."

"Oh, well, I don't want to intrude on your time with him. I can take a look at the plans, or even take them back to my cabin, then meet up with you tomorrow to go over them." His eyes shifted between Avery and Piper.

Avery threw her arms around his waist and rested her cheek against the side of his hip. "No, it's okay. I know Uncle Eugene won't care. He always says the more the merrier, right, Mom?"

Although she longed to go along with Bear's offer of taking the plans with him, she was simply delaying the inevitable—she'd have to spend more time with him eventually, so might as well do it now that he was there.

She shook her head and laid a hand on top of Avery's head. "No, he won't mind at all. In fact, he'd love another visit with you, I'm sure."

In fact, he'd talked of little else when Avery and Piper dropped by to return his plate and thank him for the cupcakes.

Bear slid her a side smile that caused her insides to tumble. She returned to the kitchen and quickly made a couple more sandwiches. Then she tossed some cut veggies, string cheese and another half a dozen cookies into the basket. She carried it to the dining room and reached for the plans the same time Bear did. His hand covered hers, and she jerked her fingers out of his grasp. "Sorry. I was just going to grab the plans and take them with us."

"Great minds. Allow me." He palmed the cardboard tube without much effort and pulled his Jeep keys out of his front pocket. "Would you like me to drive? Or should I follow and meet you there?"

The thought of sitting in Bear's Jeep… She shook her head. "I'll drive, and you can follow. Then you won't have to go out of your way to bring us back home."

He leaned close and took the basket from her, his mouth close to her ear. "You're never out of my way, Piper."

Spoken low and nearly a whisper, his words sent a shiver down her back. She definitely needed to drive with the AC blowing at max level.

Bear carried the picnic basket and cardboard tube outside and waited while she locked the apartment door and then made sure Avery was buckled in her booster seat.

They left Aspen Ridge and headed toward Eugene's farm. They turned into the semicircle driveway in front of his white two-story house with black trim, and parked. Eugene sat in a wooden rocking chair on the wide covered porch, waiting for them.

Before Piper could reach for her door handle, Avery had unbuckled her seat belt and scrambled out of the car, trailing her backpack behind her. She raced over to Eugene and threw her arms around his waist. "Hi, Uncle Eugene. Guess what?"

"I'm not a very good guesser, so why don't you just tell me."

Avery turned and pointed toward Bear getting out of his Jeep and closing the door quietly behind him. "Uncle Bear is coming on our picnic, too. I told Mom you wouldn't mind. I was right, wasn't I?"

"Yes, absolutely right." With an arm still around Avery, they moved slowly as Eugene leaned on his cane. Reaching Bear and Piper, he let go of Avery, shifted his cane to his other hand then shook the one Bear had extended. "Great to see you again, Bear."

"Thank you, sir. You as well."

Piper kissed Eugene's cheek. "Avery, Cole's

daughter, Lexi, and I made those chocolate chip cookies you love so much."

"Sounds good. Let's eat in the gazebo in the backyard."

They rounded the house, passed an immaculate flower garden with various colors of blooms and stopped at a four-sided dark wood gazebo. A round glass-topped table and four padded chairs sat in the center.

As Piper unpacked the basket, Eugene gave Bear a quick tour from where they stood in the yard, pointing out the dirt road that ran past the barn on the right side of the house and up to rows of hives sitting on the hill.

Piper called them to the table. After everyone sat, Eugene blessed the food and the company. As they dug into the sandwiches, Eugene and Bear talked about Hives for Healing, his veteran beekeeping program.

Avery pulled a book out of her backpack and leaned against Bear's arm as she pulled her knees to her chest. Holding the book in her left hand, she grabbed her sandwich.

Bear continued talking with Eugene but adjusted so Avery snuggled into his side and he draped his arm around her narrow shoulders.

Piper lowered her head and tried to focus on the ripple pattern in the glass top, but tears filmed her eyes, blurring her vision. Setting her barely touched sandwich on her paper plate, she reached for her napkin and balled it in her fist resting on her thigh.

Yes, stopping by the ranch had been a mistake.

She should've called and set up a time to meet with Bear when Avery wasn't around. Selfishly, Piper had been thinking about her own reactions about not wanting to be around him. Watching the way he drew her daughter close caused anger and resentment to burn in her belly.

Ryland should be the one her daughter snuggled against. Not his best friend, who still wanted to reclaim his career.

And now Piper would have to be "mean mom" to keep Bear at a distance.

For all of their sakes.

Chapter Five

The more time Bear spent with Piper and Avery, the more he wanted to prove he was the kind of guy she needed in her life, especially after the way Avery cozied next to him at Eugene's.

He didn't want to create more problems between them, but once again, Piper was being unreasonable.

At least Avery was distracted with Eugene's new cat—a stray who wandered onto his farm and made herself at home—to notice the tension between the two adults. Eugene sat in a chair next to them. Every now and then Bear caught him watching them. Probably being protective of Piper.

His eyes drifted toward the little girl sitting in the grass and laughing as the calico curled around her arm. Then he turned his attention back to her mother and scrubbed a hand over his face. "Listen, Piper. I understand the original plan was to go with four cabins, and I'm not saying we need to scrap that idea. After looking into material costs, I'm simply suggesting an alternative to help keep some of our expenses down and maybe even offer another option to our guests."

Piper sat at the table, arms folded over her chest, and bounced her knee. Lines deepened between her brows as her mouth tightened.

"So you're suggesting yurts. What are they again?"

The way she spit out *yurt* caused him to roll his eyes. But he tendered his tone and forced patience back into his voice. "They're cylindrical-style dwellings that are built on a raised platform with a deck to prevent rain and snow from settling underneath. Instead of a foundation, they need concrete footings poured for anchoring. Waterproof canvas like what's used for tents is stretched over a wooden frame and held in place with wooden lattice walls. Yurt kits can be purchased and assembled, but we can also price it out to see if gathering our own materials would be a better option."

Piper pushed to her feet and waved her hand over the plans unrolled on the table.

"We just paid to have an architect design the cabins with everything you and your family wanted to be included. Now you want me to ask him to design a yurt?"

Bear laid a hand on the plans. "We'll keep these because the cabins will happen. But we may need to do this project in phases as we generate more income. Let's do some research, come up with a few ideas then present them to my family for their input. I'm not saying do away with the cabins. I'd like to offer another option as well. Besides, a yurt is more of an open-concept design, anyway."

"With circular walls, won't decorating be a challenge?"

"Not really. You're the creative one. I'm sure you will come up with something pretty awesome. Let me show you a few pictures." He pulled out his phone and typed *yurts* in the search bar. He stood close enough to her to feel the heat from her arm against his and smell the floral scent of her shampoo. He pulled his focus back to the screen and thumbed through some of the exterior images. "These are just a snapshot, but it will give you an idea of what I'm talking about."

She took his phone from him, her fingers brushing against his, then held it closer to her face. The lines between her eyes softened as she looked at him in resignation. Handing back his phone, she shrugged again. "Well, it's your family, so they're going to go with your idea."

"Piper, this isn't a contest. The cabin designs are great. You did a wonderful job working with the architect. And if that's the avenue my family wants to take, I'm totally on board with it. I know this idea is sudden, and I'm sorry if you feel like I'm springing it on you. I talked to a couple of friends recently who spent a week camping in a yurt and they really enjoyed it. When they learned about our guest-ranch idea, they suggested it as an option. I did a little online research and figured it wouldn't hurt to toss the idea out there."

She turned to the window and folded her arms over her chest once again. Then she faced him. "You're right, Bear. But I don't want to pay someone to design a yurt yet. I'll do some research, too. We're meeting with your family on Monday, so that doesn't give me much time to pull some ideas together. Maybe an hour or two after church tomorrow. I thought we had a plan already, and I was all set to move forward."

Maybe he should've kept his mouth shut and stuck to the plan. But he hadn't expected to receive so much flack for offering a suggestion.

He reached for her hands and gave them a gentle squeeze. "We do have a plan. And we can move forward. I'm not trying to stand in the way of that. I simply want to consider additional options." How many different ways did he have to say the same thing?

"Okay, fine. Let's move on. I need to get Avery home and in bed soon." She pulled her hands out of his grasp and dropped them at her side, then returned to the table. She reached for the plans and started to roll them together. Then she stopped and smoothed them back out again.

"Oh, I almost forgot." She trailed a finger along the edge of the guest-ranch property. "We need to ensure all paths leading to the sites are clearly marked and maintained. I want to talk to Brad, Pete's nephew, who will be the contractor on this project, about landscaping the paths and turning them into usable gravel roads so we don't have guests getting lost and wandering off."

"And ending up in my front yard." He shot her a grin.

Her lips curved up as her eyes slid back to the plans laid out on Eugene's table. "Yeah, there's that, too."

"Dad and Lynetta promised this wouldn't interfere with my privacy."

"Yes, we want to protect that, but we can't put a bubble around the guest ranch. What are your thoughts about filling in that path that I took to your place?"

"Fill it in how?"

She lifted a shoulder. "I don't know... Off the top of my head, I'd suggest reseeding the dirt path and throwing in a lot of wildflower seeds so it doesn't appear to be a viable walking path. Or if you wanted to keep the path, maybe install a gate between the two trees. Or if you wanted your privacy protected that much, you could pay to have a fence installed around your property."

He grimaced. "I'm not installing a fence that blocks my view of the water. That's why I built my cabin there. And that's the trail I take while riding, so I really don't want to fill it in."

"Then maybe a gate with a private-property sign is the best way to go."

"Maybe. I know we're in this together, but what are your expectations of me for this project? I really don't mind lending a hand now and then, but with the ranch and Victor's rodeo school, I don't have a lot of time to wield a hammer or paintbrush."

She waved away his words. "No worries. Like I said, your uncle Pete's nephew Brad will be the contractor on the project. His crew will handle the construction. I believe you're basically to oversee and check in on their process. I'll handle the interior of the cabins…" She paused and made a face. "Or yurts. It's all under control."

"That's one thing I admire about you—you always appear to have things under control."

"Yeah, well, appearances can be deceiving. I have to keep it together for Avery's sake. I can't afford to fall apart. I'm all she has."

"That's not true, and you know it. I'm always here for you, Piper."

"I appreciate that, Bear. I do. But it's not that simple."

"No need to complicate things."

Even as the words came out of his mouth, he knew just how wrong they were. His relationship with Piper had been complicated from the moment she chose Ryland over him. And now with Ryland gone, she'd made it clear about his place—or lack of—in her and Avery's lives. She wanted nothing to do with the rodeo, and that included him as long as he was considering going back to bull riding.

He didn't blame her for not wanting to open her heart again to another cowboy, but until Ryland had been killed, she loved the rodeo. Holding Avery as a toddler on her lap, she'd cheered loud for her husband during his events. But his death changed all of that. And changed them. Again, he had to decide which dream he wanted…needed more—her or bull riding—because he couldn't have both.

Piper's coffee maker chose the worst time to die. She needed a heavy dose of caffeine if she was going to make it through the day.

She'd spent half the night tossing and turning, replaying Bear's words without allowing them to work their way into her heart. She'd finally fallen asleep in the early hours and slept through her alarm. Or else she turned it off in her sleep. Avery had woken her in a panic and then it was a mad dash to get her daughter to school on time.

So yeah, it hadn't been the best start to her day. It could only get better. Or at least, that had been her hope until she looked at her phone and found a text from Bear, asking if she could meet him, his parents, Lynetta and Pete at the ranch.

After shifting the engine into Park and turning off the ignition, Piper gripped the steering wheel, then blew out a steadying breath. She tossed her keys into her purse and grabbed the still steaming to-go cup she'd grabbed from the diner before heading to the ranch.

As she strode up the walk toward the timber-and-stone ranch house, a flock of black-and-white hens hurried past her. A warm breeze brushed over her face, carrying the scents of the fields. In the distance, a horse whinnied.

She lifted her hand to knock on the solid door, but before her knuckles could connect with the wood, the door opened. Bear stood in the doorway wearing a blue T-shirt, worn jeans and socked feet. Mrs. Stone had a strict no-boots-allowed-in-the-house rule.

"Hey, Piper. Glad you could make it." His mouth set in a grim line.

She raised an eyebrow. "Everything okay? I admit—I was a little surprised to receive your text."

He stepped back and waved a hand into the house. "Come inside, and we'll catch you up to speed."

She stepped over the threshold, and for a moment, wished she'd worn something other than her yellow The Clean Bee shirt and jeans. But she was on her way to work after their meeting. It would have to do.

The scents of fresh coffee and fried bacon

lingered in the air. Piper's mouth watered, and her stomach growled. She hadn't taken the time to grab breakfast with the chaos of her morning.

Hopefully, Bear hadn't heard. She slid a sideways glance at him only to see the corners of his downturned mouth.

Her heart pinched at whatever was weighing him down.

They headed into the kitchen, and she found Deacon and Nora Stone sitting next to Lynetta, who was shredding a tissue, and Pete. Leaning against the counter, Wyatt, Macey and Cole cupped their hands around filled coffee mugs. Their conversations stopped once they saw her.

Her stomach tightened.

The men stood, and Deacon waved a hand to an empty chair next to Lynetta. She took it and leaned close to her friend. "What's going on?"

Lynetta cupped her hand over Piper's and gave it a light squeeze. "You'll hear soon enough."

"Good morning, Piper." Nora left the table and returned with a plate piled with muffins the size of Piper's fist, a stack of napkins and another cup, which she set in front of Piper. Then she reached for the half-full coffeepot. "Would you like some coffee?"

Piper lifted her to-go cup. "Thanks, but I'm good for now. I may need a refill soon, though."

"Just yell when you're ready." She replaced the coffeepot on the burner, then returned to the table.

Bear took an empty seat between Piper and Nora and nodded to his dad. Deacon pushed to his feet once again and stood behind his wife, his hands resting on her shoulders. "Thanks for coming on such short notice. Unfortunately, I have to be the bearer of bad news. Pete's nephew, Brad Murphy, who was going to head up our construction, was in a serious accident last night on his way home from a job. A couple of his crew were with him. Brad's been airlifted to Durango for head injuries. Sadly, one of his guys didn't make it."

Piper sucked in a breath and grabbed Lynetta's hand. She leaned forward and looked at Pete. "Pete, Lynetta, I'm so sorry."

Pete nodded. "Thanks, darlin'."

Lynetta squeezed her hand, her eyes shimmering. "We won't be able to begin as we'd hoped. Pete and I are leaving later this afternoon and heading to Durango to be with Pete's sister and Brad's family. Nora's agreed to mind the diner while we're gone, and Pete's line cook will cover the back of house."

"If there's anything I can do, please let me know."

"Thanks, I appreciate that."

"Brad had planned to give us a discount on the labor in exchange for advertising on our website. Other contractors are booked solid until the snow flies. So it looks like the guest ranch is put on hold for now." Deacon rubbed a hand over his face. "Bear and Wyatt, we need to consider options, maybe selling off a chunk of land or some cattle to cover the costs for the winter."

The heaviness in the room pressed on Piper's shoulders. She could understand their frustration. Her heart ached at the deep furrows trenched in Deacon's forehead and the tears swimming in Lynetta's eyes. Not to mention Bear's tight mouth, Wyatt's downcast eyes and the way Nora traced the rim of her untouched coffee. They simply wanted to finish what their parents had started. To continue their legacy of hospitality... Isn't that what Bear had said?

She rested her elbows on the table and pressed her fingers against her eyes. The rest of Bear's conversation filtered through her head. Piper dropped her hands in her lap and straightened. "What if we don't have to put it on hold, after all?"

Deacon lifted his head and looked at her. "What do you mean?"

"I received the plans from the architect on Friday and shared them with Bear on Saturday. He'd suggested another idea in addition to the cabins. We've done some research and planned to share everything with you this evening." Piper retrieved her tablet from her purse and pulled up her research notes. She turned the screen toward the other adults. "I admit to knowing nothing about construction. Brad and his crew had been hired to construct the cabins, but what if we could work around that? Bear had suggested something called a yurt. While I wasn't too thrilled about the idea at first, I've been doing some research since then, and it may be a feasible solution."

Bear pushed his chair back. Standing behind her, he held out a hand toward the tablet. "May I?"

She placed it in his warm palm.

He tapped on the screen, then turned it sideways. "Here's a video I found talking about the affordability of a yurt. To be honest, it slipped my mind after receiving the news about Brad. We may not be able to build the guesthouse and cabins by ourselves, but from what I read, we can put up the yurts on our own."

"I'm sure a few guys on my crew wouldn't mind some side work." Cole headed to the coffee maker and refilled his cup.

Piper caught his eye and mouthed, "Thank you."

He responded with a wink.

For the next few minutes, they passed around the tablet, stopping and starting the video that showed constructing a yurt from a kit.

Deacon handed the tablet across the table to Piper, then nodded to Bear. "Could the two of you get together and come up with a cost analysis? And find out how long it would take to receive the yurt kits? Maybe we could start there and see if it's worth the investment to move forward. I'll talk to Aaron Brewster, our attorney, and ask him to see what we need as far as permits go. Brad had planned to take care of all of that for us."

Macey set her cup on the counter and moved to the large calendar hanging on the side of the fridge. "Here's something else to consider as well—we'd planned to begin construction this fall so we'd be ready to open early next year. If these yurts don't take more than a weekend to put up, then we could do a soft opening for hunters, ice fishermen and those who may be attending WinterFest.

Everly and I can brainstorm some winter family activities and add them to the website."

"That sounds great, Macey." Piper twisted and looked up at Bear. "You free tonight?"

"For you, of course." His eyes darkened as a smile formed on his lips.

She ignored the way her heart stumbled against her rib cage. Turning back to his family, she nodded. "I'll make some calls today, and we'll have some figures for you tomorrow."

Bear squeezed her shoulders. As his family's resignation morphed into hopefulness, she had a renewed excitement to work on the project again, to be a part of something that would benefit others.

But it would also mean another evening with Bear. And another sleepless night as she tried to reconcile his growing presence in her life…and her feelings for him.

Chapter Six

Piper couldn't get Deacon and Lynetta's faces out of her mind. Even though she still wasn't certain about the yurt idea, it allowed the family to move forward with their plans.

Once she finished cleaning the apartment above the diner, she'd head home and make the promised calls to have something to share with Bear when he showed up later.

She wiped down the cabinet fronts, then opened the doors and cleaned the empty shelves. She left the doors open to air them out and moved on to polishing the fronts of the appliances and the counters. She swept the eat-in kitchen floor, then mopped it quickly. After rinsing the mop and bucket, she cleaned and dried the stainless steel basins and faucet. Then she moved into the living room and did a quick but thorough dusting. Grabbing her bottle of vinegar water, she sprayed the window overlooking Main Street and shined the glass. She dusted the baseboards and gave the carpet a quick vacuum, then went into the bathroom. As she finished cleaning and mopping, her phone timer chimed.

Just in time.

She moved to the kitchen sink, slid off her wedding band and set it on the counter. Then she washed her hands thoroughly and dried them.

She reached for her ring.

Instead of sliding it onto her finger, she turned and pressed her back to the sink. Holding the thin band in her hand, she looked at it, remembering the day after her eighteenth birthday when twenty-year-old Ryland, decked out in his clean jeans, freshly pressed plaid shirt and favorite boots, had repeated the vows in his shaky voice, then slid the ring onto her finger.

She had worn a white sundress, her pregnant belly quite evident, but she hadn't cared. She was going to marry the man she loved and have the kind of family she'd always wanted.

And she had. For three short years.

For the first time in a long while, she allowed the tears pressing against her eyes to slide down her cheeks. Her fingers tightened around the gold band that Ryland had bought with his first rodeo winnings. She pressed a fist to her mouth and cried for what should have been.

After a final shudder of her chest, she wiped her eyes with the back of her hand and then held out her hand to slide the ring back onto her finger.

But instead, she slowly lowered her hand, and with an aching heart, she slid the thin gold band into the front pocket of her jeans until she could put it in a safe place for Avery someday.

It was time.

Time to let go of the past and embrace what the future held for her and for Avery.

With a final swipe over her face, she stowed her cleaning products in her The Clean Bee tote. She gave one more final look to the small apartment that had once been home after her mother had kicked her out upon learning she was pregnant at seventeen.

Satisfied with her work, Piper turned off the light and closed the door quietly behind her. She locked the door, then hurried down the back steps behind the diner. Tapping the remote on her key chain, she unlocked her SUV and dropped the bag on the back seat.

Hot and sweaty from her marathon cleaning session and her head aching from her crying jag, Piper headed into the diner for iced tea to go and swallowed a groan.

Sheila, her mother-in-law, sat in the first booth by the door with her best friend, Barb. Careful not to chip their perfectly manicured nails, they held their diner mugs as if they were fine porcelain.

Sheila caught Piper's eye, nudged her friend's hand and set her cup on the table. "Good afternoon, Piper."

"Sheila. Barb."

"So sorry to hear about the zoning for the guest ranch." Sheila shot her a smirk.

"I don't know what you're talking about." Piper shoved her left hand in her pocket, not ready to have another unpleasant conversation with her eagle-eyed mother-in-law.

"Oh, haven't you heard? Some concerned citizens have voiced a complaint with the zoning board about what the Stones want to do with the ranch."

"Why would anyone be concerned? Their project doesn't affect anyone except them and their guests."

Barb patted her hair and sniffed. "Well, maybe people are still upset because the Stones wouldn't sell their land to Wallace for that strip mall."

Piper lifted a shoulder. "They need to get over it. That land has been in the Stone family for decades and Crawford was underhanded in the way he tried to acquire it."

"Even if it was for the good of the community?"

"You and I know Wallace Crawford serves himself first and anyone else second. He wasn't thinking about the community. He had dollar signs in his eyes."

"Well, you're entitled to your opinion, I suppose. You may want to check with the Stones before you consider moving forward with their so-called guest ranch."

Gritting her teeth to prevent from creating any more friction with her mother-in-law, Piper forced a smile. "I need to get back to work. Have a good day, ladies."

Piper strode to the breakfast counter as Lynetta pushed through the kitchen door. She held out the keys to the older woman. "The apartment is cleaned and ready for your renter to move in. May I have an iced tea to go, please?"

Lynetta pocketed the keys, then reached for a paper cup, filled it with ice and set it under the drink dispenser. She handed it to Piper. "Thanks so much, love. So sorry for the last-minute request but I haven't had time to get up there after our last renter moved out."

Piper peeled the paper off her straw, stuck it through the lid and took a long drink, refreshing her dry throat. Then she tossed a couple of wrinkled dollars on the counter and pushed them toward Lynetta. "Thanks. It wasn't a problem and took no time at all."

Lynetta ignored the money and glanced at her watch. "Someone's coming in an hour to look at it. Pete and I are putting any rental money toward the guest ranch so we want to keep it rented as much as possible. But with needing to head to Durango this afternoon, we're scrambling a bit."

Piper leaned over the counter and wrapped her arms around her friend. "Take a deep breath. Everything will work out. Isn't that what you always tell me? I planned to head home to do some research, but I have my laptop in my car. I can hang out here and take orders or run the register if you need to head home for a bit. Even if it's just to catch your breath."

"Thanks, sugar. I'll admit it's been a day, but I need to keep going. I appreciate the offer, though."

"If you change your mind, you know how to reach me."

"I appreciate it. Let me write you a check before I forget."

Piper waved her hand and shook her head. "No way. I did this as a favor—one friend helping another. It's the least I could do after all you've done for me over the years."

"That's not how to run a business, giving away your services for free."

"Oh, yeah? How much for this iced tea?" She held up the cup and nodded toward the money that Lynetta had pushed back toward her.

Lynetta made a face. "That's different and you know it."

Sheila's shrill laughter climbed down Piper's spine. She glanced over her shoulder as the two put their heads together. Piper turned back to Lynetta and lowered her voice. "So when I came in, Sheila and Barb insinuated there was something wrong with the zoning for the guest ranch."

Lynetta rolled her eyes. "Those two have been stirring up trouble since high school. You'd think they'd grow up already. When Deac called Aaron Brewster about permits and all that, Aaron mentioned some people had voiced complaints about the guest-ranch proposal. Brad had already filed for the permits. Since we're not doing cabins just yet, Aaron will look into what changes need to be considered for the yurts. I don't understand all of it, and Aaron told my brother not to worry about anything. He'd handle it…and the complaints. Sour grapes, if you ask me."

"I'm sorry. I know that's the last thing you and Pete need to deal with. How's Brad doing? Any word?"

"He's stable. There's some swelling on his brain so they're watching that. His mother's a hot mess. Pete's been on the phone with her since we left the ranch." Lynetta pulled out a tray of silverware and a stack of napkins. She gathered a knife, fork and spoon, and rolled them in the paper napkin. Piper sat on a stool in front of her and did the same. They dropped the wrapped utensils in an empty basket.

"While I was cleaning your apartment, Cole texted to say Heath has a crew who can build the platforms. He also offered to help with acquiring any necessary permits. He said they can pour the footers as well."

Lynetta's face lit up as she pressed her hands against her chest. "What an answer to prayer! I'll be sure those boys get free meals when they come in."

"I don't think they are expecting that. We'll have to see what they're charging and compare it to Brad's quote."

Again, Lynetta waved away her words.

"Doesn't matter. We'll make it work. God will provide."

Piper always admired Lynetta's faith that God would work things out for them. Even though her friend had had her own share of struggles, her faith never wavered.

What would it be like to have faith like that? What would it be like to have complete trust that things would work out without knowing what the future held? Even the idea of letting go caused an ache in Piper's chest. She wasn't close to having a trusting faith like her friend, and she had no idea how to even begin.

All Bear had to do was keep his head down and mouth shut. Just answer the questions asked and the scheduled meeting with the rodeo association board would be over. Then he could head back to the ranch and move on with his day.

Leaning back in his chair, he sat at the polished table with his hat on his left knee and his hands folded. Across from him, Dalton McNeil, Rex Nelson, and Beau George, founders of the rodeo association board, tried to level him with their brow-heavy stares. But after his years of facing angry bulls, he could handle their glares. Victor Flynn, another founder but also his friend, shot him a compassionate look.

Dalton dropped his pen on the table. "So, you're saying you've changed?"

"Yes, sir."

"In what way?"

"I did the anger management counseling that was required. I've kept to myself, working the ranch with my family." He nodded toward his mentor. "Now I'm helping Victor with his Lil Riders group."

"I heard about your recent run-in with my son."

"I wouldn't call it a run-in, sir. We had a conversation, and that's it."

"You didn't threaten him?"

Leave it to Chet to embellish the truth.

"No, sir. He tried to goad me by stating he could make or break my career. But then my attention was diverted elsewhere."

"By saving Healy's girl."

"Yes, sir. She nearly stepped out in front of a car, and I pulled her to safety."

"You have a history with her parents."

"Her father, Ryland Healy, was my best friend. I've known her mother most of my life."

"I'm going to ask again—you didn't threaten my son when you saw him in front of Blake's?"

"No, sir. My problems with your son are in the past."

"The past has a way of rearing its ugly head, though."

"Only if you let it."

"So you're able to let bygones be bygones?"

"Yes, sir."

McNeil scraped a hand across his chin. "I have to say, I expected you'd be a bit more talkative than you have been. Do you even want to return to the rodeo?"

"Yes, sir. More than anything. But past experience has taught me how easily my words can be twisted. So I figured the fewer, the better. For the past five years, I've done everything necessary to prove I'm worthy to climb back onto a bull. All I can do is wait for your decision."

"All right, then." Dalton stood, rounded the table and stretched out his hand.

Bear pushed to his feet and shook it. Then he shook the hands of the other men as well.

"We'll have an answer within the week."

Bear swallowed the frustration lining his throat. He'd hoped to walk out of there with a decision today because the wait was grating on his nerves. But there wasn't anything more he could do. Bear settled his hat on his head and nodded to them. "Thank you. I appreciate your time."

Pivoting on his booted heel, he headed out the door. Outside, he blew out a breath. Sunshine struck him in the eye. He slipped on his sunglasses. After checking for traffic, he jogged across the street and reached for the diner door as it flung open.

A woman barreled into him. "Oh, excuse me. Sorry."

He reached out to steady her, and she looked up. "Oh, hey, Bear."

"Hey, Piper." His breath caught. He swallowed quickly, then jerked his head toward the open door. "Want to head back inside and grab a cup of coffee?"

"Actually, I just finished drinking an iced tea. I need to head back to my house and look into that cost analysis your dad asked about. But I do want to share a couple of things with you, if you have a minute?"

"A minute? For you, I'll give you two."

She shared the briefest of smiles, which he'd take, and held the door while she headed back inside. She grabbed an open booth near the counter, and he slid in across from her.

Her eyes glided over his face. "You look… nice. Kind of dressed up, actually."

He tried to hide his surprise and pleasure

at her compliment, and glanced down at his pressed shirt, clean jeans and polished boots. "Thanks. I had a meeting with the rodeo association concerning my possible reinstatement."

"Oh."

The single word spoke volumes, reminding him of the distance between them, so he didn't bother to share anything more. It would drive them further apart and he wanted her closer to him.

Bear turned his cup over as the server approached their table with a full pot of coffee. After she filled his cup and took Piper's order for ice water, he added milk and stirred. "So what did you want to talk to me about?"

"It's not a big deal, really. I just wanted you to know Sheila and her friend were complaining about the guest ranch and mentioned there may be zoning concerns, but Lynetta and your dad are handling it with Aaron Brewster."

"Thanks for keeping me in the loop. I'm not worried."

"Plus, Heath Walker, Cole's boss, has a crew who can help. Cole said he'd get the footers poured for the platforms."

"I can give them a hand with those."

Piper pulled out her phone. "What else?

Oh, yes, you may be able to save some material costs by taking down some trees on the ranch and having them milled."

As she held her phone, he glanced at her hand. For a moment, he couldn't figure out what was different. Then he saw it—the band of pale skin where her wedding ring had been.

"Your ring."

"Excuse me?"

"You took off your wedding ring."

"Oh." She set her phone on the table and rubbed her thumb over her finger. "I, uh, just did a little while ago." She pointed to the ceiling. "I cleaned the apartment above the diner, then washed my hands when I was done. I took my ring off, but instead of putting it on my finger, I slid it into my pocket."

"Why?"

Eyes still focused on her bare left hand, she shrugged. "It was time to put it away. Save it for Avery. She may want it for sentimental reasons someday."

He reached across the table and gave her hand a gentle squeeze. "That was a brave thing to do."

She looked at him and scoffed as her eyes watered. "I don't feel very brave."

He wanted to lift her fingers to his lips and brush a kiss across her knuckles, but he removed his hand from hers and reached for his coffee cup instead. "I think that's what courage is all about—not feeling strong or brave about something but doing it anyway. How are you feeling about it?"

She drew her shoulders up and dropped them slowly. "I don't know. My hand feels a little naked, and part of me feels like I'm betraying my husband."

"Ryland wouldn't want you to live in the past. He'd want you to move forward. To be happy. And maybe even find love again someday."

With him, but of course he couldn't say that. Not yet, anyway.

"I don't know. Maybe I used up my happily-ever-after already and I won't have a second chance at love."

Her words spoken so quietly pierced his chest. What could he say to promise her that wasn't the case? She wasn't ready for any sort of emotional declaration from him.

He understood what a huge step removing her ring meant for her. And maybe even for him. Even if she wasn't ready to admit it to herself. Like with the council's decision, he'd wait and bide his time because he felt in his heart his dreams were about to come true.

Chapter Seven

If Bear were being honest, he was going to miss overseeing Victor's Lil Riders group. Giving up an hour or two for the past few Saturdays hadn't been much of a sacrifice. Now that his friend had returned to Aspen Ridge, Bear would be handing the reins back over to him.

Victor had asked him to stay on as his assistant, and Bear promised to consider it, especially since Gavin had voiced during one of their sessions he was getting too old to be chasing kids around the arena.

While Bear wanted to say yes, he needed to make sure he wasn't taking on something he couldn't follow through with, especially with working the ranch and helping Piper with the guest ranch.

So if this was his last day, then he wanted

to make their last time together fun. He enjoyed seeing their excitement over learning new skills. Plus, he got to hang with Gavin. The colorful character kept him grinning.

He rubbed his hands together. "All right, riders. Line up. We're going to divide into two groups—five-and six-year-olds with Mr. Copeland and seven-and eight-year-olds with me."

As the kids divided according to their ages, a black Mercedes barreled down the drive, sending up dust, and parked near the arena.

The driver's-side door opened, and Sheila Healy stepped out, wearing a pressed blouse, jeans and heels. She slid her sunglasses on top of her head, gave him a little wave then opened the back door.

Avery scrambled out dressed in jeans and a pink T-shirt. Two neat braids bounced against her shoulders as she raced to the fence, waving to him. "Hi, Uncle Bear."

Bear turned to Gavin. "Be right back."

The man shot him a two-finger salute. "Do what you gotta do."

Bear strode across the arena and met Mrs. Healy and Avery as they reached the gate. He gave one of Avery's braids a gentle tug. "Hey, Bookworm. What's going on?"

She flashed him a huge toothy grin. "Nana said I could come to rodeo school."

"Is that so?" He raised an eyebrow and looked at Mrs. Healy. "Is Piper aware of this?"

Mrs. Healy lifted her chin and pressed a tight smile in place. "Avery is in my care Saturday mornings, so I'm giving her permission to attend."

"Mrs. Healy, we need Piper's permission in order for Avery to stay. You can't go behind her back, especially knowing how she feels about having her daughter enrolled in any aspect of the rodeo." He pulled his phone out of his back pocket. "I'll call her, and if she gives verbal permission, then Avery can stay. But then we need a form signed by Piper allowing her to participate."

Avery tugged on her grandmother's arm. "Nana, you said I could come."

Closing her eyes, Mrs. Healy scowled at Bear, then smoothed her face into a smile when she faced her granddaughter. "Yes, I did. But Barrett feels the need to call your mother."

Avery lowered her head and kicked the toe of her boot against a clump of grass. "She'll say no. She doesn't want me to have fun like the rest of my friends."

Mrs. Healy lifted her chin and glared at Bear as if to say, *See?*

He placed a hand on Avery's shoulder and

gave it a light squeeze as he tapped a thumb on Piper's number in his call log.

The phone rang and rang until it went to her voice mail. "Hey, Piper. I'm at the ranch. Give me a call."

He pocketed his phone and turned back to them. "No answer."

The woman rolled her eyes and crossed her arms over her chest. "You didn't have to call her, you know. I'm not doing anything wrong. What harm is it in having Avery here?"

Glancing at Avery, who looked like she was about to cry, he lowered his voice. "Piper has made it clear that she doesn't want Avery around the rodeo. Yet you chose to bring her anyway. Did you think Avery wouldn't say anything to her mother?"

"I just don't see what the big deal is. If Ryland were here, you know he would be fighting her on that."

"If Ryland were here, it wouldn't be an issue. But it's because of Ryland's death Piper doesn't want to lose her only daughter as well."

"Well, you and I both know if she keeps such a tight hold on her, Piper's going to lose her only daughter anyway."

"Mrs. Healy, Ryland was like a brother. Losing him gutted me. So I can only imagine how you must feel. But you also have to look at it from Piper's point of view. And she is Avery's mother. If you want to have a good relationship with either one of them, you need to respect that."

For Avery's sake, Piper tried to maintain a decent relationship with her in-laws, but they needed to stop undermining her authority.

"I want what's best for my granddaughter. What's the harm in riding a stick horse with her friends?"

Avery clutched the rails as she watched the kids laughing as they rode stick horses around the arena. The sad look on her face slammed Bear in the chest.

"No harm, I guess." He dragged a hand over his face as his gut tightened. Then he moved over to Avery. "Hey, Bookworm. Want to horse around with your friends?"

She shot him a look brighter than a sunbeam and scrambled off the rail. "You mean it?"

"You promise not to get hurt?"

She crossed her heart. "I promise."

Against his better judgment, he opened the gate. She ducked under his arm and raced over to her friend Casey. Gavin found her a stick horse, and she galloped around the arena with her friends.

Mrs. Healy strode over to him, arms crossed over her chest and brow raised. "See? What did I tell you?"

Before he could answer, a familiar silver SUV came up the drive and braked next to Piper's mother-in-law's Mercedes.

Piper stepped out of her car, rested her arm on the open door and whipped off her sunglasses. Her eyes narrowed as her lips thinned. She slammed her door, the sound echoing across the arena.

She blew out a breath and flexed her fingers as she marched toward them.

Bear nodded to her. "I just tried to call you."

"I was driving and hit a dead zone. Once I had service, your call flashed on my dash. I was close enough to the ranch and decided to drop in. And maybe just in time, too." She folded her arms over her chest and jutted her chin. "Why is my daughter in the arena with the kids from Victor's group?"

"Don't start, Piper. They're riding stick horses in a circle. What's the harm in letting Avery join them and have some fun for a change?" Sheila waved a hand toward the arena.

Keeping a tight smile in place, Piper glanced at Avery laughing with her friends, then returned her attention to her mother-in-law. "I don't want Avery to have anything to do with the rodeo."

"We live in a ranching community. Do you really think she's going to go the rest of her life without being exposed? You're keeping her away from everything that her father loved. Rodeo is in her blood and you know it." Sheila's voice rose, which caused some of the kids, including Avery, to stop what they were doing to see what was happening outside of the fence.

Shifting his feet, Bear stuffed his hands in his front pockets and cleared his throat. "Ladies, maybe you'd like to continue this discussion away from listening ears?"

Piper shot him a poisonous look. "You knew how I felt, yet you let her join anyway?" Before he could respond, she turned back to her mother-in-law. "I'm Avery's only surviving parent and have to do what I feel is best to keep her safe. Even if that means keeping her away from the sport that killed her father."

Dragging her stick horse behind her, Avery left her friends and headed for the gate.

"Now you're being ridiculous. She's not jumping on the backs of bulls at the age of seven." Mrs. Healy scowled and shook her head.

Piper fisted a hand on her hip. "Remind

me—how did Ryland get started with the rodeo?"

Mrs. Healy waved a hand toward the arena. "Doing the same program Victor has been teaching for over thirty years."

"Exactly. This is where it starts, isn't it? I need to keep my daughter safe."

"Then you might as well move away because the more she gets involved in school and with her friends, you will not be able to keep her away from horses, ranching or even the rodeo until she graduates."

"That's going to happen sooner rather than later." Piper sucked in her lips and scrunched up her face as if she hadn't meant to share that.

"What's that supposed to mean? Are you actually thinking of moving?"

Avery pushed through the gate, dropped the horse and hurried over to Piper. "Mom, I don't want to move away. I wanna stay here. With Nana. And ride horses with my friends. Uncle Bear will keep me safe." She peered up at him with pleading eyes that reminded him of her father. "You'll protect me, won't you?"

He crouched in front of her and ran his thumb over her cheek. "With everything I have, Bookworm."

Avery turned back to her mother. "See,

Mom. My friend Casey from school is in the class. And we were having fun."

"I don't know, Ave."

"You're so mean!" Tears slid down Avery's cheeks as she raced to the Mercedes and yanked the door open. Mrs. Healy shot Piper a disgusted look, then followed her granddaughter.

The door slammed, and Piper jumped. Anguish twisted her face. Then she ground her jaw and glared at him. "She has no idea how danger can wrap itself up in such a fun package. You know, I'm not surprised she tried something like this, but I expected better from you. You know how I feel about this."

Bear held up his hands. "I know, Piper, and you're right. I tried to call to get your verbal permission. When I couldn't get a hold of you, Avery's puppy dog eyes got the best of me."

"Doesn't matter. You should've abided by my wishes." She covered her face with her hand and shook her head. "I don't know what to do. I don't want to deny her fun and time with her friends, but you know how I feel about this."

He should've trusted his gut and stood up to Mrs. Healy, but part of him agreed with the older woman. Truly, what was the harm?

But now he had Piper mad at him. He needed to choose his words carefully.

He grabbed the back of his neck. "Listen, Piper. You're right, and I'm sorry. For what it's worth—Avery spent less than ten minutes with her friends. However, you are her parent, so the final decision is up to you. You may want to consider talking to Macey or Everly. Or even my mom. All of us kids have gone through Victor's program when we were younger. Mallory has given permission for Tanner to attend. Cole promised Lexi she could do it after she turns five. I do know Victor has tight safeguards in place to protect the children. He does a lot of practice drills that make it fun. Today, we are having a stick horse relay race. Not much harm in that."

"What about when she wants to ride a horse? Or be like her dad and get on the back of a bull?"

"Well, I can tell you this, the rodeo association does not allow seven-year-old bull riders. So I think she's safe for this year."

"This isn't a joke, Bear."

"I'm not laughing. She's already been on a horse during our family's trail ride a few weeks ago. My family takes this stuff seriously as well. We live in a ranching community, so she's constantly exposed to this kind of environment. Be sure you're not allowing your own fears to get in the way of doing what is best for your daughter. Another option would be to sign her up for a trial class. Victor offers three classes for parents to see if their kids will even like it."

Piper stepped back and folded her arms over her chest. "Will you be here?"

"Victor's home, so he'll be taking back the class."

"After today, you won't even be there to watch over her?"

Bear rubbed a hand over his jaw and turned his attention toward the kids racing around the arena. Then he shifted his gaze to Piper. "He asked me to take over for Gavin as his assistant. If you want Avery to do a trial period with Victor, then I'll do it and be at every class to watch over her."

Piper glanced at Sheila's Mercedes. "I don't want either of them to think they're getting their own way."

"Ignore her and focus on what's best for Avery."

Piper dropped her hands at her sides. "All right. Fine. She can stay today, and I'll sign whatever paperwork Victor needs for her to do a few more classes."

As she walked toward the car to share

the news with her daughter, Bear blew out a breath.

A step in the right direction. If she was willing to work through her fears for her daughter, maybe there was hope for him.

Piper wasn't a wimp by any means. Cleaning houses was hard work. But volunteering to help assemble yurts called on muscles she hadn't even known she had. Tomorrow, she'd pay the price for her charitable heart.

When Cole's crew showed up one man down, she heard herself volunteering to help before her brain had time to protest. Her cousin put her in charge of carrying lumber milled from Stone River Ranch trees to each site so they could get the platforms built.

Once they'd decided to go with the yurts, Deacon, Bear and Wyatt had spent some time with Cole to determine their best options. They cleared the area of brush and debris and trimmed a few trees so the yurts could face the water.

She appreciated they'd taken her suggestion about that.

Cole and Bear had poured the concrete footers earlier in the week so they'd be set by the time the crew needed to build the platforms and assemble the yurts.

Long shipping crates containing the remaining yurt supplies sat next to the tree line out of the way.

Piper rubbed the back of her leather-gloved hand across her sweaty forehead, then reached for the two remaining boards and carried them to the last site.

She grabbed her lower back and stretched to loosen the tightening muscles. A hot bath was going to be necessary before she crawled into bed tonight.

The whine of the saws and popping of the air hammers pierced the air. Someone hooked up their phone to an external speaker and country music streamed through the trees.

She forced herself to focus on all the other activity so her wandering eyes wouldn't settle on the way Bear's T-shirt tightened across his back or the way the muscles in his arms and shoulders strained as he settled the boards in place.

She wanted to stay mad at him over the whole debacle with Avery joining the Lil Riders group, but while talking with Avery, she remembered Bear had protested to her mother-in-law. And a talk with Macey and Cole had assuaged some of her fears. But not all of them. Bear's promise to protect her daughter helped.

He was becoming an integral part of their lives. When they moved to Durango, Piper worried how it would affect Avery. She didn't want to admit she'd been wondering the same for herself, too.

Tires crunching on the gravel road drew her traitorous attention away from Bear. Nora and Macey exited Nora's SUV. Macey opened the lift gate and removed a folding table while Nora retrieved a large wicker basket covered with a checkered cloth.

Macey carried the table to a clearing close to the water, opened it and set it in place. Then she ran a shaky hand over her pale face.

"Hey, you okay?" Piper moved over to her and placed a hand on her friend's back.

"Yeah, I'm fine. Just had a bit of a rough morning. Must be a bug or something. My stomach's been a mess for a couple of days, and I haven't been able to keep much down." Macey yawned and covered her mouth. "And I've been so tired the last week or so."

"Aww, Mace. Sorry to hear that." Piper glanced at Cole, who was helping Deacon with the final board on their platform. "Cole seems to be okay. How's Lexi doing?"

"Oh, she's just fine. Seems like I'm the only one who caught it. I just don't know where, though. We haven't been around anyone who was sick." She shrugged. "I don't know. Maybe it's a touch of food poisoning or something."

Nora laid out the checkered cloth on the table, and Piper straightened it on her side. Then Nora pulled a plastic container of sandwiches from the basket and set it on the table. She removed the lid and the scent of egg salad drifted toward them.

Macey closed her eyes and clutched her stomach. "Excuse me." She rushed away from the table toward the tree line.

Piper grabbed a water bottle from the cooler Bear had brought that morning and hurried after her friend. She paused at her car, opened the glove box and pulled out a couple of fast-food napkins.

She thrust them into Macey's hand, uncapped the water bottle and held it out to her. "Drink some water. It will help you to feel better."

Still bent at the waist, Macey shook her head and held up a hand. "I'll just throw it up in a few minutes. I haven't been able to keep anything down for a few days."

Piper screwed the cap back onto the bottle. "Want me to take you home so you can go to bed?"

Macey shook her head again, then stood.

She wiped a hand across her mouth. "Can't. Everly has Tanner, Mia and Lexi right now. I'm supposed to help Mom set out lunch, then I'm heading back to the ranch to take the kids to our place so Everly can go out with some of her friends from school."

Piper glanced at her watch. "I need to get Avery in an hour. How about if they come to my house for a while? Then you can get some rest."

Macey ran another shaky hand over her face, then nodded. "Okay, yeah, that will work." She reached for Piper's arm. "Please don't tell Cole about this. You know how he stresses when Lexi gets sick. I don't want him to worry about me, too."

"He's your husband, Mace. You can't keep this from him."

"I know. And if it continues, I'll give my doctor a call. I just don't want to sound the alarm for no reason." She folded her arms over her chest and winced.

Piper gasped. "I think I know why you're sick."

Macey scowled. "How?"

Piper grinned and brought her mouth closer to Macey's ear. "Because I had very similar symptoms...right before learning I was pregnant with Avery."

"P-pregnant?" Macey's eyes widened. "But I can't be pregnant. We've been married only a month."

"Ever hear of a honeymoon baby?"

Covering her eyes, Macey shook her head.

"You're tired and nauseous. When you crossed your arms over your chest, you winced. Feeling a little tender?"

"I figured it was PMS. Cole is going to freak out." Then her eyes sparkled as her mouth widened into a smile. "We hoped to wait a year at least."

"Maybe God had different plans for your family." Piper jerked her head toward the crew. "Want me to fetch that unsuspecting cousin of mine?"

"Would you mind?"

"Not at all." She handed the water bottle to Macey. "Take this in case you change your mind."

Piper headed back to the work area and made a beeline for Cole, who was filling a plate. She leaned in and whispered to her cousin, "Hey, let me hold your plate a minute. I think Macey needs you."

Cole looked up, a frown on his face as he scanned the area. "Where is she? She okay?"

Piper nodded toward the tree line. "She will be. But she needs you."

Without another word, Cole thrust the plate at Piper and broke out in a run toward Macey.

"What's that all about?" Bear nudged her shoulder.

"Macey's not feeling well."

"That stinks. I hope she's not pulling Cole away. We need all the help we can get if we're going to finish on time."

"Nah. Just needs a minute with him."

Cole reached Macey and took her in his arms. She must have whispered something to him because he jerked back and looked at her. She nodded at something he said, then he let out a whoop, pulled her close again and twirled her around.

Piper swallowed a laugh. Silly guy. He wouldn't be doing that for the next few months if he knew what was best for his wife if she's getting nauseous this early.

Piper's eyes warmed with tears as Cole caressed Macey's cheek then cupped her face and kissed her. Taking her hand, Cole returned to the table with Macey.

"Hey, guys, I'm going to take off for about an hour or so, but I'll be back. Mace isn't feeling well, so I'm going to run her home."

Nora reached for her daughter. "Honey, why didn't you say something? Want me to take you back to the ranch?"

Leaning into her husband, Macey shook her head. "Thanks, Mom, but Cole wants to take me home. I'm sure I'll be better in no time."

As they walked away, Bear took a large bite of his sandwich and shook his head. "Those two…"

"What about them?"

"Nothing. They're just… Why couldn't Mace head home by herself?"

"There are times when a woman needs her husband."

"Yeah, I guess."

"Wouldn't you do the same thing?"

"Maybe. Although if I were Cole, I'm not so sure I'd be heading back to a bunch of sweaty guys when I could be snuggling with my wife." He flashed her a direct look with such intensity that Piper tore her gaze away.

Her eyes drifted to the dust trails that were the remaining evidence of Cole and Macey's departure.

She could count on one hand the number of times Ryland had stayed home when she'd got so sick while pregnant with Avery. Usually, he made sure she had what she needed, then headed out to meet up with his rodeo buddies. At the time, she hadn't dwelled on it because at least he still wanted to be with her.

She envied Cole and Macey and the way he always put her and Lexi first. What would it be like to be with someone who put her first? Someone who chose her over anyone else?

Someone like Bear?

Chapter Eight

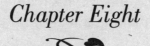

Bear hadn't expected Piper to show. But now that she had, he wanted nothing more than to prove they could have a good time together without arguing.

He had gone to the early church service with his family and was surprised to find her already there. He mentioned his plans to take a hike in the San Juan Mountains and invited her to join him. Since Avery was with her grandparents and wouldn't be home until later that afternoon, Piper agreed, taking him a little by surprise.

He needed to send Mrs. Healy flowers or a gift basket or something for this opportunity. But she was still ticked at him for trying to call Piper last weekend when she brought Avery to the Lil Riders group without her mother's permission.

But that had worked out for the best. Avery loved hanging out with her friends yesterday before Bear had left to work on the yurts with his family. He'd kept his word to Piper about watching over her.

Right now, though, his main goal was to keep from making a fool of himself on the trail.

He parked his Jeep in the parking lot and hurried around the front to open the passenger-side door.

"Always the gentleman." She shot him a smile that hit him straight in the heart.

"Absolutely." He grinned. He grabbed his backpack out of the back seat and slid the straps over his shoulders.

Before meeting him at his cabin, Piper had changed into olive hiking shorts with pockets on the sides, a light purple T-shirt, walking shoes, and she tied a sweatshirt around her waist. Her hair had been pulled back into a ponytail, and he had to force himself not to touch the soft-looking skin at her neck.

He tossed her a can. "Spray your arms and legs so you don't bring home any ticks or other creatures. Be sure to get your socks and shoes, too."

She gave him what he called the mom

glare. "This isn't my first hike, Bear. I grew up here, remember?"

"Of course, but it's always good to be safe."

Once they both sprayed themselves, he tossed the can back inside the Jeep. He lifted his arms and pointed his fingers toward the trailhead. "Let's take the trail to the lake. It's not a bad stretch."

She slid her arms into her small backpack. "I'll follow your lead."

If only she would do that in life as well. Then he wouldn't have to fight his feelings for her. She'd fall in line alongside him.

They followed the path through a grassy meadow dotted with wildflowers. Every so often Piper stopped, pulled out her phone and took a picture.

"You were great yesterday, by the way. You're certainly not afraid to get your hands dirty."

She shot him another look he couldn't quite decipher, but if he had to guess—his comments pleased her. "I get my hands dirty every day. It's part of the job."

He lifted a shoulder. "You know what I mean."

"When one of Cole's guys had to pull out at the last minute, I wanted to pitch in so we could stay on schedule."

"My family really appreciates all you're doing."

"Don't think I'm being all magnanimous about this. I have skin in the game, too, you know."

He laughed and nudged her shoulder with his. "Oh, check out the cute girl and her five-dollar words."

Her cheeks darkened. She pulled her water bottle from the mesh side pocket of her pack, removed the lid and pointed it at him. She squeezed and shot him in the chest. He jumped back but not before it hit his chin, soaking his neck and shirt. "Hey, no fair."

She laughed, and the sound sent a spark through him. She could spray him as much as she wanted if it meant she'd laugh like that again.

Thankfully, the sun overhead in the cloudless blue sky would dry his shirt in no time.

Their path twisted uphill over boulders the size of tractor tires. Bear held out his hand more than once to help her with the climb. Each time she took hold, he hoped she wouldn't let go. But once she found her footing, she trekked the rest of the way on her own.

Their trail flattened and cut through a forest of aspens and Douglas firs. They came to an overlook.

Bear uncapped his bottle and chugged half of it, then poured a little in his hand, which he washed over his sweaty face and neck.

Piper rested against the metal railing lining the cement foundation and used the edge of her T-shirt to wipe off her forehead. Waterfalls roared out of the gorge and tumbled down into the lake below.

"Absolutely gorgeous." Shielding her eyes with her hand, she turned her back to him and gripped the railing.

He moved beside her and drank in her side profile, memorizing the soft curves of her jaw and her slender neck. "I couldn't agree more."

She glanced at him and then looked away quickly, her cheeks darkening once again.

She sighed, almost wistfully. "My mom used to bring me here when I was a kid. We'd have a picnic and forget about our problems."

"You don't talk about her much."

Piper shrugged. "What's the point? She wants nothing to do with me. To her, I am the shameful daughter who got pregnant as a teenager. After Ry's funeral, she moved out of state without telling me, and I haven't seen her since. She hasn't made an attempt to see Avery."

"Her loss. If God can forgive you, then why

can't she?" Bear pressed his back against the railing and looked at her.

"Who says God has forgiven me?"

Spoken almost as a whisper, he wasn't quite sure he'd heard her correctly. He scowled. "Seriously, Piper? You really believe that?"

She picked up a leaf, tore it into pieces and dropped them over the railing. "Ry and I made a mistake, and he paid the price."

Bear pushed away from the railing and dropped his hands to his hips. "Wait, what? Paid what price?"

Piper turned and linked her arms over the top bar. She kicked her toe against the pavement. "I guess I figured God was angry like my mom for what we'd done, so to punish us, He let Ryland die."

Bear's heart nearly melted. He cupped her cheek. "Piper, sweetheart, that's not how God operates."

She pushed his hand off her face and glared at him. "Oh, so you know the mind of God?"

"Not even the slightest. But I can't believe that a graceful, merciful God would be so angry at what happened that He would give you such a miracle as Avery and then punish you with Ryland dying."

"Well, apparently my mother serves a different god because that's what she told me at Ryland's funeral. That it was my fault my husband was dead."

Bear swallowed the anger rising in his throat. Slamming her mother's distorted thinking wouldn't change anything.

"I've had my own issues with God since Ryland's death and being thrown out of the rodeo association, but I still stand by the notion that He did not kill Ryland to punish you. We don't know why He allowed Ryland to die but the Bible does tell us He will turn brokenness into beauty and there will be joy in the morning."

Piper pulled her water bottle out of the pocket, took another swig—without squirting him this time—and then stowed it. "Let's finish our hike so I can get back before Avery gets home."

Bear waved a hand. "Lead the way. I've got your back."

They walked in silence for the next fifteen minutes, then came to another clearing. At that moment, Piper's stomach growled.

He laughed. "Maybe now is a good time to stop for lunch."

"Lunch?"

"Sure. Why not?" He slid his backpack off his shoulders and unzipped it. He pulled out a blanket, shook it and laid it flat. Then he

grabbed a couple of turkey and Swiss sandwiches, two Honeycrisp apples, two bottles
of water and a container of chocolate cupcakes his mother had given him yesterday,
and placed them in the middle of the blanket.
He patted the empty space across from him.
"Have a seat."

She settled on the blanket and crossed her
legs. "Wow, Bear. I didn't expect this."

"Hiking always makes me hungry." He patted his backpack. "If this isn't enough, I have
a couple of protein bars and some trail mix,
too."

"This is plenty. You're full of surprises,
aren't you?"

"That's me. Mr. Unexpected." He handed
her a sandwich, and she took it.

She unzipped the top, then she lifted her
eyes, a serious expression radiating from
them. "Yes, I'm beginning to find that out.
You're not the Bear I used to know."

Bear straightened and set his sandwich on
the blanket. "I hope that's a good thing."

She pulled out her sandwich and took a
bite. "Yes, most definitely a good thing."

He finished his sandwich, then reached for
the container of cupcakes. He opened them
and pushed them toward her. "Mom made cupcakes yesterday with Tanner, Lexi and Mia."

"I love how your family has embraced Cole's daughter, Lexi." She finished her sandwich, then grabbed an apple.

He took a cupcake and peeled away the liner. "Why wouldn't we? She's family."

"Sure, but she's not yours biologically."

"Maybe not by blood, but she is by heart, and that's all that matters. Besides, Macey's adopting her. She's one of us now."

Eyes downcast, she twisted the stem off her apple and tossed it in the grass. "So you'd be willing to take on a child who wasn't yours by birth?"

He stilled, trying not to let her words set off fireworks in his chest. He finished his cupcake in two bites, then wiped his fingers on the edge of the blanket. He reached for her hand. "Yes, absolutely. If I loved someone and they had a kid, then I'd love 'em as if they were mine."

"You've always had a big heart, Bear. I don't know if that's a good thing or a downfall."

"I'd rather have a big heart and get hurt than not have a heart at all."

"You're a rare breed."

"Maybe you just haven't been around the right people. Stick with me, kid." He rubbed his knuckles across her chin in a playful jab.

She laughed again and bit into her apple.

Leaning an elbow on the blanket, he stretched out and nudged the cupcake container closer to her. "You better get a cupcake before I eat all of them."

She held up her hand. "No cupcakes for me. I don't eat them. Thanks, anyway."

He sat up. "What? Are you kidding? Cupcakes are nearly the best thing on the planet. They deserve their own food group. Especially these chocolate ones with Mom's homemade frosting."

Piper lowered her eyes and dropped her half-eaten apple into her empty sandwich bag.

What has he said now?

"Piper?"

She sighed, looked over his shoulder and dragged a hand over her hair. "When I was ten, I tried to make cupcakes for my mom's birthday. I mixed something up, and they were horrible. Mom was so mad that I had wasted food like that. I felt so ashamed. The next day, on my way home from school, I stopped at the bakery and used my birthday money and bought two decadent, beautifully frosted cupcakes. They had swirls of frosting at least two inches thick and lots of sprinkles and they were the nicest ones in the case. When I took them home, Mom snapped at me for being so wasteful with my money. Then she said they had too many calories and she wouldn't eat one anyway. I threw the bag away and went to my room. I cried myself to sleep, and she never checked on me. Not once. Not even to eat dinner."

"And I take it you haven't eaten a cupcake since?"

Her eyes downcast, Piper shook her head and sniffed. "I should get over it, right?"

Bear stood and walked around the blanket. He pulled Piper to her feet, then drew her against his chest. "I'm so sorry she treated you that way. You're such a great mom to Avery."

"I promised God if He let my baby live, then I would do everything in my power to be the best mother I could." Her words were muffled against his T-shirt.

He drew back. "Live?"

"Avery was born premature and had breathing issues. She spent time in the NICU. I begged God to forgive me for getting pregnant, and if He healed my sick baby, then I'd be the best mother possible so she didn't have a childhood like mine." A tear drifted down her cheek.

"Babe, I'm sorry. I had forgotten about the struggles surrounding Avery's birth. God longs to shower you with His blessings. Not because we deserve it, but because that's who He is."

"You really believe that?"

"I'm trying to. My dad's tried to pound that into our heads for years. One of these times it's gotta stick, right? My family's had its share of hardships but my dad doesn't allow those to shake his faith."

Piper wiped a finger under her eyes. "Yeah, I can see that in Lynetta as well. Must be a family trait. She's been the mother I always wanted. She and Pete have helped Avery and me more times than I can count."

"That's my aunt. She couldn't have kids, so she's cared for kids in the community as if they were her own."

"She denies it, but I think she and Pete helped pay my tuition."

Bear wasn't sure how to respond. He didn't want to reveal his secret and change what was growing between them. "You don't say."

"I didn't have enough for my last year and planned to drop out, but Lynetta convinced me to register. She promised God would provide. And He did...most likely through them. She wouldn't accept money when I tried to pay her back. Said it wasn't hers to take."

Bear tightened his hold on Piper and kissed

the top of her head. "Accept the gift and just know someone really wanted to help you."

"I'll pay it forward someday, to help a single mom trying to make it on her own."

"I'm sure you will. You're a generous person. My family can attest to that with the time you've spent helping us get the guest ranch off the ground."

"It's been my pleasure. Mostly."

"We'll write a recommendation or referral or whatever you need because we wouldn't have got this far without you."

"Sure you could have. I'm nobody special. Anyone could've done what I've been doing."

Bear stroked his thumbs over her cheeks and directed his eyes at her. "When are you going to realize just how special you are?"

She didn't say a word. Very slowly, her hand crept around the back of his neck. Standing on tiptoe, she brushed her lips across his.

His brain stalled for half a second, then he drew her close and returned the kiss. She tasted of apples and peppermint lip balm.

He'd been waiting for years to have her in his arms, and it was worth the wait. Hopefully, she didn't regret it.

Piper should've said no when Bear asked her to go hiking. But she'd just had another disagreement with Sheila about keeping Avery longer than scheduled and didn't want to go home to an empty apartment.

And now she found herself in his arms— the one place she hadn't expected to be. Nor was it a good idea. Was it?

She wasn't even sure anymore.

But she couldn't find the strength to move. Did she really want to? She learned long ago that what she wanted needed to take second to what needed to be done.

She hadn't been in a man's arms since Ryland. She missed the physical contact. But that wasn't a good enough reason to throw herself at Bear.

She kissed him. Not the other way around. She had no one to blame but herself.

She slid her hands over his shoulders, down his arms and gripped his elbows. She tried to step back but he tightened his hold.

He pressed his forehead against hers. "Now that I finally have you in my arms, do you really think I'm going to let you go?"

She took in a deep breath, inhaling his closeness that smelled of soap, sunshine and fresh mountain air.

"Bear…"

"Piper, don't overthink it." His words, spoken low and oh, so close, ignited something she wasn't ready to define.

Holding on to his arms, she laughed. "Have you met me? I'm the reigning queen of overthinking."

He touched her chin. "Trust me. I will never hurt you."

Trust. She wanted to believe him, but Ry had said the same thing so many times, and she'd had to learn how to live without him.

"You say that now, Bear, but people hurt one another all the time."

"Not intentionally. Not those they care about."

"Stop caring about me."

"That's like telling me to stop breathing. No matter what happens, I'll never stop caring about you or Avery. You're both locked in here." He slapped his hand over his heart.

"You need someone else in your life to care about. Have you even dated anyone since Staci dumped you? The last five years have been hard with losing your best friend, career and fiancée in one painful shot."

"Staci wasn't much of a loss. I was young and stupid. We dated less than six months. I got caught up in the fun of our relationship without thinking through my proposal. She moved on once she realized I was nothing more than a disgrace. To be honest, I don't even think about her. I wasn't that broken up when she ditched me."

"You a disgrace? Seriously? How is that even possible? You're such a boy scout."

"Boy scouts have flaws. Two words—Chet McNeil."

"That guy's a jerk."

"Both times I've had a run-in with him, I've been called a disgrace."

"Both times? I only know about the fight from five years ago. You got into it another time?"

"When we were kids, Chet and I ended up being in the same swim class. I was in the locker room and he started hassling me about my size. I was a puny kid at the time. He said I was too slow and not as strong as the other swimmers. Because of me, our team took second instead of first. He started calling me names and pushed me. I shoved him back and he slipped on the wet floor. He hit his head on the bench and needed to get stitches. When Dad picked me up and found out what happened, he was furious. Said my behavior was a disgrace. I tried to tell my side of the story, but he wouldn't listen. Then Coach wouldn't let me finish my classes."

"Ouch. I'm sorry."

Bear lifted a shoulder. "It is what it is. I worked hard to make my dad proud so I wouldn't bring shame on the family. Blew that by punching McNeil in the jaw."

"And that's when Staci broke up with you, too, right?"

"Something like that. Said being around me reflected poorly on her. Whatever. I knew she wasn't right for me, but I guess I got caught up in the idea of being in love with her."

"Her loss." She gave him a playful slug. "You're a catch."

He held out his arms. "Here I am. Catch me."

As much as she wanted to walk back into his arms, she shook her head. "You don't want me."

He took a step toward her. "You sure about that?"

She pocketed her hands so she wouldn't reach for him again. "Staci wasn't the one who got away?"

"We shouldn't have dated let alone got engaged." He shook his head and rubbed a hand over the back of his neck. "The one who got away married my best friend."

Spoken low, she ran his words over in her head. *Married his best friend... Oh.*

Oh.

Her head jerked up. He looked at her with

such tenderness that her breath caught in her chest.

"Bear..."

He lowered his head, his lips claiming hers very gently, almost tentatively as if gauging her response.

She was tired of overthinking, of playing it safe. She leaned into his embrace and allowed him to draw her close. She'd face the consequences tomorrow, whatever they may be.

Chapter Nine

When Dad invited him for breakfast, Bear hadn't expected company. Especially members of the rodeo council.

He'd walked into his parents' kitchen to find Dalton, Beau, Rex and Victor sitting at their table.

What were they doing here? And why did he feel like he'd been sent to the principal's office?

Had he known they had company for breakfast, then he would've taken the time to change out of his jeans with a rip across the thigh and ragged T-shirt he'd thrown on to do morning chores. He was here now and couldn't do anything about it.

"Morning, gentlemen." Bear headed to the sink and washed his hands. Then he shook hands with the men drinking Mom's coffee.

She offered him a cup. He pressed a kiss against her cheek. "Thanks, Mom."

Dad gestured to the empty chair at the table. "Have a seat, Bear."

Trying to hide his curiosity, Bear pulled out the chair.

"I'm sure you're wondering what we're doing here." Dalton leaned forward and rested his forearms on the table.

Still holding on to his coffee mug, Bear leaned back and nodded. "The thought crossed my mind."

"We have a proposition for your family."

"What kind of proposition?"

"One that could benefit all of us. Did y'all hear about the fire at the rodeo arena last night?"

Bear exchanged glances with Dad, then shook his head. "No, I didn't hear anything. What happened?"

"We're not sure yet. Fire inspector came out this morning, but we won't have his report for a week or so. He does suspect foul play. The judges' box, animal holding pens and a section of the old bleachers are nothing but ashes."

"So, what does that have to do with us? You don't think I had anything to do with it, do you?" He wasn't taking the fall for this.

Victor held up a hand. "No worries, Bear. We're not here to blame you. We're here to help you."

"Help me in what way?"

"You're building a guest ranch to generate income for your ranch, right?" Victor twirled his spoon between his fingers.

"That's correct."

"With the Aspen Ridge Rodeo coming up, we need a place to hold it. Since the fire inspector suspects arson, our property is considered a crime scene and they won't allow us to rebuild right now. We were considering spreads in the area with enough land and yours came to mind."

Dad raised his eyebrows. He stood and refilled their coffee cups before dumping the remainder in his own. "So you want to use Stone River for your rodeo?"

"Yes, we'd like to do a short-term lease on your property to hold the rodeo. If we cancel, then we lose funds for our fire department and our police department."

Bear swirled the remaining coffee in his cup. "I'm still waiting for a decision regarding my suspension, which was supposed to happen within the week of meeting with you. Wouldn't it be kind of strange to hold the rodeo on Stone River property when I'm banned?"

"About that…" Dalton glanced at the other members of the council. "We took a vote and decided to lift your suspension and give you probationary status."

Bear swallowed the anger choking his throat. "What was the vote?"

"Excuse me?"

"Did you all vote for those terms?" Bear glanced at Victor, who gave him a slight shake of his head.

"Well, no. The vote to lift your suspension was unanimous. The probationary vote was three to one."

He figured as much. Victor wouldn't have voted against him.

Dad pushed away from the counter, stood behind Bear and rested his hands on Bear's shoulders. "If you want to lease Stone River property, then Bear's name is cleared completely. No probationary status. The suspension lifts without conditions. In fact, you will make a statement to the press regarding the unfounded accusations that led to this ridiculous ruling in the first place."

"Now, Deacon, come on. You know as well as I do, he hit my boy on national TV."

"And you know as well as I do that your

son was bad-mouthing Ryland Healy's wife. I don't condone violence, but I don't approve of sexual harassment, either. We can't choose our sins, Dalton. Your boy has been out of line for years and you turn a blind eye. My son defends a lady's honor and he loses nearly everything."

Dalton's face flushed as he ran a finger between his neck and his shirt collar. He pushed back his chair, stood and hitched up his jeans. Glancing at Mom, he gave her a nod. "Thank you for the coffee, Nora." He jerked his chin toward the other men. "I think we're done here."

Victor lifted a hand. "Park it, Dalton. We're not going to jump up just because you don't like what Deacon had to say. You, as well as everyone else around this table, know it's the truth. Chet's been out of control for years and you just let him run wild. This whole America's Cowboy thing has gone to the kid's head and other people are paying the price for his mistakes. So, unless you want the whole rodeo to fold, I suggest you sit down and let the Stones have their say."

Bear wanted to pump his fist in the air, but he stayed quiet. He lifted his chin to Victor, who shot him a wink. It felt good to have others on his side.

Bear tuned out Dalton's bluster and focused on the other council members. "Should we come to some sort of agreement, what are you looking for?"

For the next hour, they hashed out the details of what was needed—an arena for the events, room for vendors, animal holding pens and plenty of parking. The fire department would deliver portable bleachers and restrooms. The police department would handle the security and help with parking. The rodeo council would ensure any property damages were repaired to the Stones' satisfaction.

Dad looked at Mom and turned his attention to Bear. "What do you think?"

Bear lifted his shoulder. "I think we should run it by the family. It's going to affect all of them. Then we need to determine which piece of property would be the best location."

"Are you sure about this?"

Bear set his empty cup on the table. "Sure, provided my suspension is lifted and I get to ride."

Dalton's head jerked up. "Ride? No one said anything about that? You haven't been a part of the association for five years."

"If you want to use Stone River Ranch, then those are our conditions." He pushed back his chair and stood. He rounded the table and kissed his mother's cheek. "Thanks for the coffee, Mom. I need to head to the barn."

Bear headed to the utility room where he had toed off his boots.

Finally. For the first time since the whole debacle happened, he felt like he had gotten his say. And now he may have the opportunity to do what he had been waiting to do for five years—climb on the back of a bull.

Piper's face swam through his head. What would she say when she heard the news?

Bear didn't have to guess. He knew. And any chance he had with her hinged on his decision to ride or not.

Kissing Bear had been a mistake. Piper should have known better. She was allowing history to repeat itself, and she wasn't the only one who was going to get hurt this time. She had to think about Avery, too.

She hadn't seen Bear in three days. Not since their hike.

She expected him to call, but his number never flashed on her screen.

Was he ghosting her? Was he regretting his actions as well?

Oh, well. She was better off anyway.

Tell that to her heart.

Falling in love with a cowboy just led to

heartbreak. Experience had been a bitter teacher. Besides, she had more important things to think about right now.

Now that the yurts had been assembled and the bathrooms installed, she needed to get them ready for Macey to take pictures for the website.

They had decided to build a room within the center of the yurt to include a bathroom. Cole's crew had built a ladder against the back wall and added a loft bedroom with two twin beds above the bathroom. The main floor had a small kitchen area with an island for prep or for sitting.

On the other side of the wall, they had chosen a coffee-colored microfiber convertible sofa that faced the large paned windows that overlooked the lake. A couple of side tables, a low bookshelf and a wall-mounted TV created a cozy living space. A privacy wall sectioned off the primary sleeping area, which held a queen-size bed, nightstand and a small chest at the foot of the bed.

The yurt closest to the road had been made accessible with ramps, wider doorways and enough space to maneuver a wheelchair, walker or other mobility device. Cole's crew added an accessible shower with safety features. Instead of a loft bedroom, they added two double beds to the main sleeping area.

With the curved lattice walls, decorating could be a challenge. Piper wanted to focus on the natural elements used in the construction of the yurts. The lattice and the two-by-fours used to support the walls had been stained to bring out the wood grain.

As she wandered through the yurt, she dictated notes into her phone about what needed to be purchased. Staying with the Western theme, she, Lynetta and Nora decided on different colors of plaid for each yurt.

An engine sounded outside, and a dog barked.

Piper closed the dictation app on her phone, headed for the door and stepped out onto the porch.

Dakota jumped off the back of the Gator and raced over to her. She brought her knee up as he jumped, placing his front paws on her leg. She wrapped her arms around him and ran her hands through his thick coat. "Hey, buddy. How's it going?"

Bear slid out from behind the wheel. Wearing a faded blue T-shirt with two holes in the side, jeans with a gash across the thigh, and his Broncos hat shading his face, he looked deliciously scruffy.

Her heart picked up speed as he sauntered toward the deck.

He lifted a hand. "Hey."

"Hey, yourself." She stowed her phone in her back pocket and then folded her arms over her chest. "Where have you been?"

She hated the nagging tone in her voice.

Bear shoved a hand in his front pocket. "The ranch. How about you?"

"Too busy to use the phone?"

A slow grin spread across his face. "Did you want me to?"

She shrugged. "Do what you want. I don't care."

He took another step toward her, and she backed up toward the door. "So, if I had used my phone, what would you have wanted me to say?"

"Bear Stone, you've never been at a loss for words."

"Except when I'm with you." He reached for her as her back bumped against the door. He stood so close she could see the gold flecks in his green eyes, and he smelled of sweat, hay and fresh air. It took everything within her power not to inhale deeply.

He pressed his left hand against the door frame above her head. With his other one, he touched her chin, then ran his thumb along the edge of her jaw.

She swallowed. Hard. "How… How did you know I'd be here?"

"I didn't. Kota and I were heading back to my place after having coffee at the ranch house, and I saw your car. Decided to stop."

"Oh."

"How are you doing?"

"Fine. You." She flattened her hands against his chest, feeling his heart beneath her palm.

"Now? Much better." His eyes dropped to her mouth.

For as much as she wanted him to kiss her, she didn't need the complication.

She reached up and flicked his hat off his head. It thumped to the deck floor. Dakota barked.

Bear took a step back and grinned, causing the lines to deepen around his eyes. He picked up his hat and placed it backward on his head.

She used that as an opportunity to swing open the screen door and step inside the protective boundary of the yurt. She half expected to hear the door slam behind her. But when she didn't, her heart jumped again. She didn't need to turn around to know he was inside the yurt. She felt his presence.

"Place looks nice." He spoke so closely his breath feathered across her neck.

"Thanks. Cole's crew and your family did the work. I'm doing cleanup and making sure everything is ready for Macey to take pictures for the website."

"How soon before we can open?"

Piper lifted a shoulder and shoved a hand in the front pocket of her shorts. "That's up to your family, I guess. When would you like to open?"

"By the end of the month. Maybe sooner."

"Seems doable. Why then? You have something planned?"

Bear dropped his hat on the counter and ran a hand through his hair. He leaned against the island. "I had an unexpected breakfast meeting this morning."

"With who?"

"The rodeo association council. Did you hear anything about a fire last night?"

"No, I ended up going to bed soon after Avery. What happened?"

"Apparently, someone tried to set fire to the rodeo arena, and arson is expected."

"That's kind of scary. Any suspects?"

"I don't know. The fire marshal isn't allowing anyone on the property until their investigation is complete. With the Aspen Ridge Rodeo in a couple of weeks, they won't have enough time to rebuild. The council met with Dad and me this morning to see if they could lease a portion of Stone River to hold the rodeo."

"Oh. What did you say?"

"We plan to talk to the family, but one of the conditions is they need to reinstate my membership and let me ride."

"Ride?" The word nearly caught in her suddenly dry throat. "As in a bull?"

Bear grinned at her, but she didn't find the humor. "I know my way around a horse. So no worries there."

"Knock it off. I'm serious."

He straightened and schooled his face. "So am I, Piper. You know what this means to me."

"And you know what it means to me. My husband, who was also your best friend, was killed by a bull, remember? How can you get back on one of those dangerous things? They shouldn't even be allowed."

He reached for her. "Hey, what happened to Ry was tragic. No doubt about it. But that's not the norm. Guys train for years to handle the bulls. And safety is always the number one priority."

"Tell that to my daughter, who is growing up without her father." Tears burned Piper's eyes as she gripped the edge of the island. "Why, Bear?"

"Why what?"

"Why get on the back of a bull again? What are you trying to prove?"

"That I deserve to have my career back?"

"A dangerous, reckless career."

"Piper, you're saying that only because we lost Ry. Before that, you were all about the rodeo."

"Yeah, well, grief has a way of changing one's perspective."

"I know, and I'm sorry you had to go through that. Be sure, though, it isn't blinding you."

"What's that supposed to mean?"

"If Ryland had been killed in a car accident, would you stop driving?"

"That's different."

"How so?"

"Bear, I'm not gonna argue with you. You know where I stand."

"And you know what I want."

"After the hike, I thought Avery and I were

what you wanted. I guess I was wrong." She started to walk away.

He grabbed her elbow and turned her gently toward him. "Why can't I have both?"

"Because I refuse to allow my daughter to lose someone else she loves."

Bear cupped her face. "Your daughter? Or yourself?"

She covered his hands and pulled them away from her face. "They're one and the same. Now if you'll excuse me, I need to head back to work."

She grabbed her bag off the table, flung the door open and hurried across the yard to her car. Only then, did she allow the tears to fall.

She had been a fool for falling in love with a cowboy once again.

Chapter Ten

Piper just needed to get through the next hour. Then she could figure out which direction to take.

Bear had called, asking if she could attend a family meeting at the ranch, not even bringing up their argument from the previous day. He wouldn't tell her what the meeting was about, and that was probably a good thing. Had she known they were going to discuss the rodeo, she may not have shown up.

But here she was.

And she had to decide if she was going to follow through with her word and participate in the one thing she hated most in the world—the rodeo. Or if she was going to give up her role in finishing the guest-ranch project.

Thankfully, there wasn't much left to do. The bedding had come in, so she needed to make up the guest rooms and finish furnishing the kitchen cabinets with dishes, utensils and cookware. Then she could be done and walk away.

Sitting in the Stones' living room, she felt like one of those kids' magazine puzzles—which one does not belong? She was the outsider here.

Macey and Cole snuggled in one corner of the couch with Wyatt holding his daughter on the other end. Tanner and Lexi colored pictures at the coffee table in front of them while Everly sat on the floor by her father's recliner with her elbow resting on the raised footrest. Bear stood near the stone fireplace where a fire crackled.

With the rain falling and hitting the windows, the fire made the room even cozier. Scents of brownies, freshly baked chocolate chip cookies and brewed coffee filtered through the air.

Piper sat on the edge of the chair, her hands gripping her untouched cup of coffee.

Deacon stretched back in his recliner with his hands folded behind his head, looking quite relaxed, which was quite the opposite of what Piper was feeling.

Wyatt sat his daughter on the cushion next to him and pushed to his feet. He grabbed a cookie off the coffee table and used it as a pointer as he looked at his brother. "So you're saying they want to lease our property short term to hold their rodeo?"

Still leaning against the stone fireplace, Bear shoved a hand in his front pocket. "Right, without enough time to rebuild, they have two choices—find a new venue or cancel, which takes funds away from the fire and police departments. If we say yes, then they will do a rush order and have new flyers and posters printed up. Plus, they'll spread the word through social media."

"What kind of damage are we talking? And where do you first see this happening so it doesn't interfere with the cattle?"

Deacon lowered the footrest and moved his chair to an upright position. He stood and turned to the framed map hanging on the wall behind his chair. He circled an area close to the ranch gate with his finger. "South Bend would have the easiest access from the main roads. That's why Wallace Crawford wanted to acquire that property." He jerked his head toward Macey and Cole. "But I won't do that to them."

Macey lifted Cole's arm off her shoulder and moved next to her dad. Hands on her hips, she looked at the map. "What are we talking? I mean, our property doesn't have cattle on it so the pasture is free."

"We need space for the arena, holding pens for animals, room for vendors and parking. Not to mention space for pickups and horse trailers." Bear dropped to his haunches and rested an elbow on the arm of her chair.

Macey looked at Cole. "What do you think, babe?"

He shrugged. "I'll do what's best for the family. The house is set far enough back from the road, so our privacy won't be violated."

Bear glanced at his siblings. "So we're in agreement?"

Wyatt rested his elbows on his knees and dragged a hand over his face. "Yes, I think so, as long as they follow through with repairing our property."

"Dalton said the council will cover those costs."

"Then I'm in."

Bear gave Piper's knee a gentle squeeze, then pushed to his feet. "Dad made sure one of the conditions of holding the rodeo at Stone River was that my membership was to be reinstated. Plus, they'll be releasing a statement to the press."

Piper's stomach twisted. Cupping her mug

in one hand, she stood and glanced at the Stone family. "Excuse me."

Escaping to the kitchen, Piper set her cup on the kitchen counter and gripped the edge of the sink.

"Hey."

Bear's gentle voice did little to ease the tension in her neck. She crossed her arms over her chest and closed her eyes against the mounting pressure.

"Look at me." He touched her and turned her gently to face him.

She opened her eyes. "Bear, what am I doing here?"

"I wanted you to be here so you were clear on everything that was taking place."

She waved her hand toward the living room. "This has nothing to do with me. This is between your family, which I'm not a part of."

He stepped closer and touched a loose strand of her hair. He twirled it around his finger before sliding it behind her ear. Then he trailed his knuckle along her jaw. "You could be, you know."

He had spoken so low Piper wasn't quite sure if he actually said what she thought she had heard. "Be serious, Bear."

The side of his mouth lifted as his eyes

tangled with hers. "I've never been more serious about anything in my life." He reached for her hand. "Piper—"

"Hey, Bear… Oops, sorry." Macey giggled as heat scalded Piper's face. She moved away from him and reached for her coffee cup with trembling fingers.

Bear ground his jaw and let out a breath. He pressed his back against the sink. Folding his arms over his chest, he glared at his sister. "What's up, Mace?"

"I was just going to…" She paused and waved her hand. "Never mind, forget it."

"Spit it out."

"What about doing an interview about your comeback to the circuit? But that discussion can wait. I didn't mean to interrupt. If you could come back into the living room for a minute, though, Cole and I have something to show you."

"You're not interrupting anything." Piper glanced at her watch. "I need to get going anyway."

Macey grabbed her hand. "Stay. Please. At least for a few more minutes."

"Yes, please stay." His words spoken gently and as a request touched something inside her. She wanted to. So badly.

"For a few minutes."

Piper followed Bear and Macey back into the living room. Macey sat next to Cole and grinned brightly as she touched Lexi on the shoulder. "Lexi, honey, want to show everyone your new shirt?"

"Okay, Mommy." Lexi stood from where she had been coloring and moved to Macey, who unzipped her hoodie and helped her out of the jacket. She pointed Lexi toward Nora, who sat on the other end of the couch. "Go show Nana."

Nora held out her hands. "Come here, sweetie, and let me see that."

Lexi ran over to her and pulled out her shirt.

"'I'm the big sister,'" Nora read, frowned a second, then gasped. Her hands flew to her mouth as she turned toward Macey. "You're pregnant?"

With a wide grin and shimmering eyes, Macey nodded.

Nora leaned across the cushion and enveloped her daughter and son-in-law in a tight hug. The other family members started talking at once and crowded around them, taking turns hugging the expectant couple.

Not wanting to interrupt the family, Piper returned to the kitchen and set her cup in the sink. She slipped on her shoes and headed out the door without saying goodbye. She'd catch up with Bear later. The more she stayed in their home, the more her heart crumbled into pieces.

The way they'd discussed the whole rodeo conversation so rationally and showered Macey and Cole with so much love created an ache inside her. She longed to be a part of a family like that.

What would it have been like to have understanding parents? Parents who guided instead of judged? Parents who nurtured instead of tore down? Parents who loved her unconditionally.

She had no idea, but she knew for certain that's what she wanted for Avery. When Bear suggested she could be a part of his family, well, she couldn't allow herself to wander down that hopeful path, because they couldn't be together with his dream nearly within reach.

Bear shouldn't have said yes to the interview. When his sister had suggested it, he'd had his reservations, but he'd given in for the sake of the ranch. He'd have an opportunity to share his side of the story and put in a plug for the guest ranch.

But the interviewer didn't want that.

All Tiffany or whatever her name was wanted to talk about was the tragedy surrounding Ryland's death. He didn't want to relive the past events that led to the demise of his career. He'd tried to steer the conversation back to the rodeo and moving forward, but each time she deflected with a question stirring up the past again. He was just glad it was over.

Would he always be defined by his past mistakes?

He headed out of the diner, where he'd met the reporter for their interview, and flung the door open a little too hard. He winced as it smacked against the building.

"Well, hello there. You must be in a hurry."

As he hustled toward his Jeep, Bear nearly ran into Eugene, Piper's landlord and friend. "Hey, Eugene. Sorry. I didn't mean to nearly run you down."

Eugene waved away his words. "No worries. I'm heading to the diner for some coffee. Care to join me?"

Bear glanced over the man's shoulder. "I just left, actually. Not really in a hurry to head back inside."

"Oh?"

The one syllable question tugged at Bear's gut. He rested an arm on the parking meter ticking down the minutes left in his spot. "I just did an interview for the paper."

"Judging by your tone, am I correct to assume it didn't go well?"

"She just wanted to talk about Ryland. Why can't people leave what's past in the past?"

"The past does tend to color the present."

He tucked his hands under his arms. "I get that, but why do I feel like I am constantly being defined by my past mistakes?"

"Perhaps it is a matter of perspective." Eugene picked up his cane and pointed it at Bear. "I haven't known you that long, but something tells me you're not that same man."

"I'm trying not to be."

"You should come back out to the farm one of these days. I'd love to take you on a tour of the hives and show you more about the program. Get to know some of the men. They're wrestling with some of their own past mistakes."

"I've been wanting to get back out there. Your program fascinates me. While I have no experience with the military or combat, I certainly respect the veterans and what they've gone through. They have some things in common with rodeo veterans such as brain injuries and PTSD."

"Speaking from experience?"

Bear tapped two knuckles against the side of his head. "My rock's too hard for a brain injury, but Ryland's death did mess with my head a little bit."

"In what way?"

He shrugged. "Nightmares. Stuff like that."

Eugene kept both hands over his cane as he stared over Bear's shoulder. "Yes, I get that. Death can be ugly, especially when someone so young is taken from us so tragically."

"Life-changing."

"Definitely. I lost my best friend in combat. Felt like I should've lost my life instead of him. He left behind a wife and twin girls."

Bear's chest tightened. How many times had he asked why not him? Why Ryland?

Eugene lifted his cane and pointed at Bear's Jeep. "This yours?"

Bear nodded.

"How about we go for a ride? Unless you have someplace to be?"

Bear dug his keys out of his front pocket and unlocked the doors with his remote fob. "Climb in."

Once they were seat-belted, Bear backed out of the parking space. "Right or left?"

"Turn right."

Bear followed Eugene's directions until he pulled into the parking lot of his family's church. He shifted into Park and let the engine idle. "Did you need me to drop you off here?"

"No. I just figured this was the perfect place for you to find some peace."

Bear stared at the brick building with glass doors and a cross mounted on the outside wall. "Hey, man. I appreciate this and all, but I'm doing just fine."

"Are you?"

Bear flashed him a side-eye. "Are you a therapist of some sort?"

Eugene laughed. "After I lost my best friend and my leg in the same blast, I needed my fair share of therapy. And it helped me so much that I went back to school and got my degree in mental health counseling."

"I didn't realize that."

Eugene lifted a shoulder. "Not many people know about it. If they know you're a therapist, they tend to clam up. Think of me as a friend with a good listening ear."

Bear gripped the steering wheel. "I can see why Piper holds you in such high regard."

"She's a pretty special young lady. I heard a rumor that the Aspen Ridge Rodeo is going to take place on your family's ranch."

"Not a rumor. Dad and Dalton McNeil met with our attorney, Aaron Brewster, to finalize the details."

"You planning to ride?"

"I'd like to." He drummed his fingers on the steering wheel.

"How's Piper feel about that?"

"As well as you could imagine."

Bear wanted to resurrect his rodeo career. And now the opportunity was within arm's reach. So why did he feel hesitation? That's what he wanted, right?

He didn't need a therapist to help him discover that answer. All he needed was to look inside his heart. Which did he want more? The rodeo or Piper? Because gaining one was going to lose the other. And he had to be fine with whichever decision he made.

Chapter Eleven

Maybe Bear did have an ulterior motive. Maybe he stepped in to help Piper with the yurts so they could be done quicker. Maybe then he could convince her to take a trail ride with him.

She needed a break. They both did. So why not take one together?

"This is our last yurt?" His eyes scanned the living area she'd already set up with the dark brown couch and end tables. She went back and added an entertainment center and a wicker chest that held blankets and doubled as a coffee table.

Piper looked up from smoothing the comforter over the queen bed, blew a lock of hair out of her eyes and reached for one of the pillows she'd given him to hold. "Last yurt?"

"You know—the last one to decorate?"

She stood and pressed a hand to her lower

back. Then she wiped the back of her wrist across her forehead. "Yeah, I guess. Why?"

He lifted a shoulder. "Just wondering."

Muttering to herself, she shook her head. "We're not even close to opening. There's no plan in place. No guesthouse built. No dock for water activities."

"No worries. It'll all work out. With the rodeo happening at the end of the week, we decided to open the yurts for accommodations. The hotels in town are booked, so we can take advantage and earn some quick cash as we get the rest of the guest ranch up and running."

"I just hope it doesn't backfire." She turned back to the bed. She smoothed a hand over an invisible wrinkle, then faced him once again. "The yurts will be ready, but you're offering them a limited experience. How will that look when it comes to reviews and word of mouth? Has your family planned any activities to offer them? We haven't even come up with a solution to keep your property off-limits."

"You're worrying needlessly. Macey's handling the reservations, and she's letting the guests know we're doing a soft opening with more to come. She's offering them a sneak peek at a discounted rate along with an opportunity to come back for the full guest-ranch experience."

"Why didn't you lead with that?" A fist on her hip, she scowled at him.

He pulled out his phone and waved it at her. "I tried to talk to you all weekend, but you wouldn't respond to my texts. I called but I got your voice mail."

She moved to the window and straightened the navy curtains that matched the red-and-navy plaid comforter. "I was busy."

"Or you were avoiding me."

"So that's why you showed up while I'm trying to get everything ready?"

"I showed up to offer my help. I can do more than hold pillows."

She brushed past him. "Shouldn't you be practicing how not to get yourself killed in the arena?"

He reached for her arm. "That's why you're avoiding me? Because I want to get back into bull riding?"

"Do what you want, Bear. It has nothing to do with me." Piper pulled her arm out of his grasp and headed for the kitchen area.

Oh, this woman…

He followed her like a little puppy. "It has everything to do with you."

"Great. Then don't do it. Problem solved."

She wiped down the counter and the front of the appliances. Again.

Bear took the cloth from her and set it on the counter. Hands on her shoulders, he turned her to face him. "If I give up trying to resurrect my bull-riding career, then I have a shot with you?"

She rolled her eyes. "A shot with me? What? Are you in tenth grade or something?"

"I'm serious."

"So am I."

He jerked a thumb toward the door. "Let's take a break. Go for a ride. Talk."

"I have too much to do. I'll get the yurts finished as I promised, then I'm turning the rest of the project over to your family. There's not much left for me to do, anyway. You guys can figure out the planning of activities, create the website and social media accounts, and determine how you're going to roll out the next phase of this project."

"And what will you do?"

"Walk away. It's time." She shoved her hands in her pockets and turned her back to him.

"Walk away before you get hurt again, is that it?"

She whirled around, eyes ablaze. "What do you want me to say?"

"I want you to consider staying to see how our relationship can develop."

"We've been over this already. I cannot afford to lose another adrenaline junkie in such a risky career."

"Is that how you saw Ryland? An adrenaline junkie?"

"No, that's how I see you. Seems like you're in it for the rush."

Bear scraped a hand over his jaw. "At one time, maybe. But not now."

"What's changed?"

"Losing Ryland. I guess we thought we were invincible. Let's go for a ride. Then we'll come back and I'll help you finish. Everything will be as you would like it."

Well, not everything.

If he chose to ride, nothing would be the same again.

She dragged a hand over her hair. "Okay, fine. For an hour. Then I have to get back to work."

"Deal. Good thing I brought the horses with me. Saves time."

She raised an eyebrow. "Feeling a little sure of yourself, aren't you?"

"Nothing wrong with a little confidence."

They headed outside and Piper stopped on

the porch. Ranger and Patience, his mother's horse, were tied to the railing.

Piper glanced down at her clothes, then back at him. "I'm not really dressed to ride a horse."

He grinned, taking in her pink T-shirt, blue shorts and leather sandals. Her hair had been twisted in some sort of messy bun. "You look great to me."

He stood to the left flank of the horse and held out a hand.

She ignored his hand, put her left foot in the stirrup, reached for the pommel and threw her leg over the saddle. She pulled her sunglasses off the top of her head, slid them in place and settled on Patience like a pro.

He untied Patience's reins and handed them to Piper. He mounted Ranger and clicked his tongue. "Come on, boy. Let's take the pretty lady on a ride."

He glanced over his shoulder to ensure Piper planned to join him. Not that he expected her to ditch him or anything, but he wanted to make sure she wasn't second-guessing herself.

Something she excelled at.

If only she could see herself through his eyes. But that might scare her off if she truly knew how much he loved her.

* * *

Maybe Bear was right, after all—a quick ride would do her some good, especially if this was their last chance to be together.

Once he climbed onto the back of the bull... She didn't even want to go through thinking about that right now. She wanted to enjoy the ride while it lasted, then she'd return to finish the yurts for the weekend guests.

She still felt it was too soon to open, but they hadn't asked her opinion, so she'd stay quiet.

They rode through the grove of aspens that were beginning to turn color. Gold threading through the green reminded them warm weather was coming to an end. Especially in southwestern Colorado, where they could see snow next month.

They took the tree-lined trail along the river that fed into the lake. Sunlight streamed over the surface, turning the water into a cascade of diamonds.

The grass around the small lake had been mowed, and a couple of benches provided rest and tranquility.

"I don't think I've been on this side of the lake before. It's lovely." She shaded her eyes, then dismounted without any help.

Bear dismounted and let the horses roam

without being tethered. "The lake was quite small when my grandparents bought the property soon after they were married. Over the years, they've expanded it. I get why Dad and Aunt Lynetta want to use it for the guests, but I enjoy having my private retreat."

Piper walked to the water's edge and toed off a sandal. "The water looks so inviting."

"Feel free to step in but don't be surprised it takes your breath away."

She didn't need the shock of cold water to do it when Bear had a way of doing that all on his own...much to her dismay.

Why couldn't she have fallen for a librarian, an insurance salesman or even an accountant? Someone who didn't want to risk his life on a dangerous animal? What was it with her and cowboys, anyway?

She slid her foot back into her shoe, then made her way across the rocky shore to the grass where he waited and watched her.

Feeling a little self-conscious under his watchful gaze, she sat on the grass and pulled her knees to her chest. Shielding her eyes, she looked up at him. "Hey, this is last minute, but Avery's eighth birthday is tomorrow. We're not doing anything big but Eugene invited her to hold her party at his gazebo. She asked if I'd invite you for pizza."

He dropped beside her and rested his elbows on his knees. "Yeah, sure, of course. Tell her I'll be there."

She nodded and tried to ignore the sizzle that shot through her when his arm brushed against hers. She kept her focus on the water. "She has a few friends coming. We'll play a couple games, do an activity she picked out, then eat pizza and ice-cream cake. I invited Sheila and Ken Healy. I'm not their favorite person right now, but I'm sure they'll show up for Avery. Just wanted you to be aware."

"Not a problem for me. How are things going between the three of you?"

Piper shrugged. "They'll always be in my life and I won't do anything to keep them away from Avery. I just wish Sheila would respect my role as Avery's mother instead of undermining me all the time."

"I have no parenting skills whatsoever. Just make sure that when you're thinking of Avery's best interests, it's not because of your fears."

She bristled. "Why do you keep saying that?"

"You allowed Avery to join Victor's school, but you won't let her compete in the mutton bustin' event at the rodeo. While I respect your decision as her mother, it could lead to problems down the road."

"Please, Dr. Barrett, share your professional opinion."

He flashed her a grin. "Your sarcasm is noted. Rebellion, for one. Resentment."

Piper pushed to her feet and brushed off the seat of her shorts. "You are right about one thing—you're not a parent. And you're not Avery's parent. I'm the one who has had to care for her and protect her on my own since Ryland died." She waved her arms as her voice rose. "I don't care if you and the rest of Aspen Ridge think I'm being overprotective. That's your choice. But I will still do what I feel is best for my daughter. Maybe it would be for the best if you didn't come for pizza tomorrow, after all."

Bear rose and came to her side. He pressed a hand against her hip. "Piper, don't shut me out just because you don't like what I have to say. You are her mother, but at least consider Avery's perspective before you shut down any thoughts of her participating at the rodeo. She wants to please you, but she's also been feeling left out while her friends have been getting excited about the upcoming rodeo."

"Maybe it's time to pull her from the rodeo

camp. After all, if she's not going to compete, then what's the point of being there?"

"It gives her something different to do and allows her to interact with a few friends outside of school. Shows her how to overcome fears. We all need that."

"What could you possibly be afraid of? You climb on the backs of raging animals."

"Climbing on is the easy part. Staying on will make or break you. If you do well, you're a hero. The first time you make a mistake, everyone turns against you." His eyes dimmed.

She rested a hand against his chest. "Like the fight with Chet?"

"I don't go around punching guys for no reason. The media painted me to be some sort of aggressive monster." He turned away from her and stared at the water.

She moved next to him and nudged his shoulder. "Why did you hit him?"

He shook his head and shoved his hands in his back pockets. "Doesn't matter. It's in the past now and I can't change what happened."

"It matters to me."

He remained quiet for a moment, then released a sigh. "Fine. I decked him because of you. Happy?"

"Me? I didn't do anything."

Bear kicked up a stone with the toe of his

shoe, caught it then skipped it across the surface. "Exactly. He said something about you that I didn't like. I told him to back off and he kept running his filthy mouth. I didn't think—just reacted and punched him. A reporter happened to catch it. You know the rest. I'm not proud of it."

She watched the ripples fan out across the water. Funny how one little stone could make such an impact. The weight of his response rested on her chest. Finally, she swallowed and touched his arm. "You did that for me?"

He faced her, his eyes dark and brooding. "I told you, Piper—I will always be there for you and Avery. I'll do what it takes to protect you both, even losing my career."

Piper didn't know how to respond. She'd never known the cause of their fight. Now to discover that she was involved indirectly... well, that gave her a different perspective. Sure, he'd said he'd do whatever it took to protect her and Avery, but to do it and lose his career over it...that spoke even louder than his words.

Nobody, not even Ryland or his mother, stood up for her like Bear did. He was definitely one of a kind.

Question was—what was she willing to do about it?

Chapter Twelve

Bear was out of his element.

When Piper mentioned a few friends, they had different ideas of what that meant. Eight girls, including Avery, crowded around a table under Eugene's gazebo, laughing and giggling as they painted suncatchers. Piper had enlisted Macey to take pictures, so Cole and Lexi showed up as well.

He'd admit Piper knew how to throw a fun bash, at least for little girls. Pink pom-pom-like streamers hung between the gazebo poles along with strands of tiny lights. Pictures of Avery from birth to eight had been printed and hung above an empty picture frame mat where her friends could write a birthday note. Bright pink bowls of M&M's, Swedish Fish and popcorn lined the table. Each of the girls had received little gift bags filled with sparkly things.

Gift bags and pastel-colored packages adorned with glittery cupcakes and unicorns sat on a table next to his oversize box. Maybe he should have asked his sisters to go shopping for him. They would've had a better idea of what little girls liked. But when he saw the white bookcase with scalloped trim, he thought of Avery right away.

Once the girls finished painting, Piper and Cole cleared the table. Piper placed the cake in front of Avery as they sang "Happy Birthday." She blew out the candles, then opened her presents while the adults sliced and served the cake.

Maybe he didn't have to stay.

She wouldn't miss him, would she? She was busy with her friends and wouldn't notice if he wasn't there.

He glanced over his shoulder toward the road. He'd leave, then text Piper later and thank her for the invite.

"Looking for an escape?"

Bear turned as Eugene approached, holding two plates of melting cake in one hand, and held one out to him.

Bear took it, careful not to drop the fork on the ground. "Adding mind reading to your list of talents?"

The man laughed as he forked his piece.

"I know what it looks like to feel uncomfortable, and you've looked over your shoulder several times now. I figured you were hoping to skip out on the party without your absence being noticed."

"Is it that obvious? I'm not sure why they invited me. I don't belong here."

Eugene shook his head and laughed. "They wanted you here. Even though Avery's busy with her friends, your presence matters to her. And to Piper, too."

"I'm not so sure about that." Bear shoved a large bite in his mouth, then regretted it as the cold hit his teeth.

"She likes you."

"She's made it clear more than once that we will not work."

"Maybe she's trying to convince herself, more than you, of that."

Bear's eyes drifted across the yard. Piper laughed at something Cole had said. She looked so happy around others and a little closed off around him. "She blamed me for Ry's death, then spent nearly five years ignoring me."

"She puts up walls for protection."

"More like a fortress. You've been good for her, for both of them."

"She's like the daughter I never had."

"Any thoughts on how I can win her over?"

"Just be patient. She'll come around."

"For how long?"

"For as long as it takes. The girl's working through some pain. Trust doesn't come easy as she's had too many people either walk out of her life or leave her in some way. I think she's afraid to give her heart to someone else and have him do the same."

"I keep telling her I'm always here for her."

"Ryland said the same thing. I think she wants to believe you, but you and Ryland were close like brothers from what I understand."

"He was my best friend. While I loved and respected him, there were also some things about him I didn't like. He didn't put Piper first. For him, it was all about the rodeo."

"What about you? Would you put her first?"

"Of course. And I've told her that. But it doesn't seem to matter."

"Actions need to speak louder than words. She's heard words all her life, but she's also seen very little follow-through. Be a man of your word and show her how you feel. Then see what happens." Eugene glanced at his watch, then clapped Bear on the shoulder. "I need to head back to the house for a meeting.

Think about what I said. You're a good man, Barrett Stone. Don't let anyone else make you feel otherwise."

Bear pondered the older man's words. Then Avery let out a squeal, pulling him from his thoughts. She raced across the yard, arms stretched out, and threw them around his waist. "Uncle Bear, I love it. Thank you so much for the bookcase."

Still holding his plate, he crouched and gave her a hug. "You're welcome, Bookworm. I'm glad you like it."

"It's perfect. Can you come tonight and put it together?"

"Let me check with your mom. This is your special day, and she might want you all to herself."

"She won't care. I'll ask her now." She pushed away from him and ran back to her mom.

Bear couldn't make out their words, but then both of them looked at him and Avery pointed. Smiling, Piper said something to Avery, who grinned and shot him a thumbs-up. Then she hurried back to her friends.

Piper headed in his direction, looking gorgeous in her flowy blouse and jeans with her hair in another messy bun. She stopped about a foot away from him and smiled. "You made her one happy little girl."

He shoved a hand in his pocket. "She deserves to be happy."

"Yes, she does." She drew in a breath and let it out slowly. "What else would make her so happy today is if you came over tonight and put together her new bookcase, which was a great gift, by the way."

"I'm glad. I was sweating it for a minute. It doesn't come with a unicorn horn or a sparkly cupcake. I was beginning to think it was a birthday fail."

"You could've given her a bag of dirt and she would've loved it because it came from you. You seemed to know exactly what she wanted."

"Now if only I could do the same with her mother."

Piper didn't respond, but was it his imagination or did she inch a little closer to him?

"What time should I come over?"

Arms crossed and hands gripping her elbows, Piper lifted a shoulder. "Whatever works best for you. I'm sure you're busy and have a lot to do."

"Never too busy for Avery." He reached for Piper's hand and gave her fingers a gentle squeeze. "Or for you."

Again, she didn't respond, but she squeezed

his fingers gently and then released his hand. She took his empty plate. "I have to get back to the girls. Let me know what time to expect you."

Maybe Eugene was right.

Maybe if he just bided his time, then Piper would come around. He was prepared to wait. However long it took.

All she had to do was get out of the car.

Every time she reached for the handle, she couldn't find the strength to open the door.

Why had she agreed to come?

Because Avery had asked her to. And she'd always show up for her daughter.

Piper wasn't going to dwell on the fact that when Bear had finished putting together Avery's bookcase the other night, he'd asked her to watch him ride. She said she'd think about it.

And she had.

She was there, but the thought of him climbing on the back of a bull turned her stomach to mush.

"Come on, Mom. I'm gonna be late." Avery tapped on the driver's-side window and called through the glass.

"I'm coming." Piper grabbed her tote bag off the passenger seat and pushed open the door.

Avery, dressed in jeans and a pink button-down shirt that matched the cowboy hat she'd received from her grandparents for her birthday, tugged on her hand, and pulled her toward the road where the arena had been set up at Stone River.

Portable aluminum bleachers rimming outside the area glinted in the late afternoon sun. White vendor tents dotted the freshly mowed pasture. Across the road, another pasture was being used for parking. Numbered stakes and yellow-vested volunteers with orange-capped flashlights guided visitors where to park. Bear suggested she park at the ranch house and walk down so she could leave if it became too overwhelming.

She appreciated his thoughtfulness.

The tang of barbecue drifted through the air, mingling with the sweet scents of cotton candy and taffy.

At the entrance table, Piper flashed Avery's badge, which allowed both of them to bypass the growing line and get in without paying.

Even though the rodeo didn't start for a couple more hours, the stands were more than half-full.

Piper pulled out her phone and sent a text to Cole. We're here. Where R U?

Three dots appeared to show he was responding. By the judge's station. In the grandstand.

Nice. One of the perks of being married into
the family holding the event, I see. :)

Clutching her phone, Piper shielded her
eyes and searched the stands. Cole waved to
her from the closed-off section of bleachers.

She returned to her phone and texted, See
you in a few. Dropping A off with the Lil Riders.

Piper thought long and hard about what
Bear had said about showing Avery how to
face her fears, so one of Piper's birthday gifts
to her daughter was registering her for the
mutton bustin' contest. Avery's squeals said
it all.

Piper didn't want to think about what could
happen if her daughter fell and broke a bone
or something. She had to let it go once Bear
promised to be there with her.

Piper dropped off Avery with Victor, reminded her to be safe and gave her a kiss,
then left on legs made of warm taffy.

The scents of the animals drifted from the
holding area. The sounds of sheep competed
with the diesel engines idling as trucks pulling trailers made their way behind the arena.

She climbed the sun-warmed bleachers and
sat in front of Cole and Macey, who cradled

a sleepy Lexi in her arms. "Hey, guys. Great seats."

"Like you said—one of the perks of hosting the rodeo. Did you get Avery checked in?"

Pasting a smile in place and clutching her stomach, Piper nodded. "She's so excited."

Cole squeezed her shoulder. "How are you doing?"

"Feeling like I want to throw up." The afternoon sun heated the top of her head, which did little to ease the tension mounting at the base of her skull.

"Hey, now. Only one of us can be sick at a time." Macey laughed behind her.

Piper slid down the bleachers so she could talk to her friend without twisting her neck too much. "How are you feeling?"

"Not bad. A little nauseous, but Cole takes good care of me with crackers and ginger ale. Cute dress, by the way." She nodded her forehead toward Piper.

Piper glanced down at her blue ruffled chambray dress she'd paired with tan ankle boots. "Thanks. In this heat, it was a cooler choice than jeans. I figured you'd be down there taking pictures or something."

Macey rolled her eyes and elbowed her husband. "I'm not allowed. Cole feels it's too risky for the baby."

Piper raised an eyebrow. "Overprotective much?"

He slung an arm over Macey's shoulders. "Say what you want, but I'm protecting my baby carrying my baby."

For as much as she wanted to tease her cousin, she appreciated his gentleness toward the ladies in his life and how he cared for them.

Her phone vibrated in her dress pocket. She pulled it out and found a text from Bear. Just saw Avery. Are you coming today? No pressure if you don't feel up to it.

I'm here. Sitting with Cole and Macey, she typed back to him.

He replied with a heart-eyes smiling emoji. I'll come to you.

Four little words, yet the impact sent her heart slamming against her ribs.

"What's got you grinning like a fool?"

Piper stowed her phone and wiped the smile off her face. "Nothing."

"Maybe my big brother has something to do with it. You two looked pretty cozy in the kitchen the last time we were at the ranch house."

Piper didn't have to work hard to tune out Macey's good-natured ribbing as her attention was drawn to the long-legged cowboy in faded jeans, a blue-and-white plaid West-ern-cut shirt and a cowboy hat climbing the bleachers with the agility of a mountain lion.

He settled next to her and smiled with watt-age brighter than the overhead arena lights. He bumped fists with Cole, gave Macey's knee a gentle squeeze then tugged gently on one of Lexi's braids. "Hey, Lexi, are you ex-cited to see Uncle Bear ride?"

She jumped off Macey's lap and stood on the bleacher in front of them and gestured dramatically. "Daddy said you're riding a bull. Won't you get hurt?"

"Nah, I'll be just fine." He grabbed her into a hug and tickled her. Then he fished some-thing out of his pocket and handed her a crin-kled bill. "Why don't you take your mommy and daddy down to Aunt Lynetta's conces-sion stand and buy a special treat?"

She opened the money and revealed a ten-dollar bill. Then she threw her arms around his neck. "Thanks, Uncle Bear. Come on, Mommy and Daddy."

Cole looked at Macey. "I think he's trying to get rid of us."

Bear cocked his head and winked at his sis-ter. "You roped yourself a smart one, Mace. Now scram."

Laughing, Macey punched her twin brother playfully in the shoulder.

Once they left, Bear turned to Piper and reached for her hand. He entwined his fingers around hers. "I'm glad you came. I know how hard it must have been to walk through the gates."

She stared at his long fingers, nicked and cut from long hours of ranching. "Of course—Avery's here. I wasn't about to drop her off and leave. Besides, I'll always show up for her."

"Just Avery?"

"Bear..."

"Listen, Piper, I know this is tough for you. I mean, man..." Still holding her hand, he rubbed the back of his neck and swallowed a couple of times. Then he blew out a breath. "I haven't set foot in the arena since Ryland died."

She dropped her gaze to their clasped hands. She'd been so caught up in her own emotions that she hadn't taken the time to think about how this return to the rodeo would be affecting Bear. "Neither have I. You doing okay?"

"I wasn't expecting the rush of memories. I can only imagine how you're feeling. That's why I wanted to check on you."

"Thanks, I appreciate it." And she meant it.

If she were being honest with herself, she'd admit the man sitting next to her had a large part to play in the reason why she showed.

Piper scanned the stands filling quickly with people. "Despite the venue change, there's been a great turnout."

"Yeah, my folks are pumped. Dalton said the council had decided to give a portion of the proceeds to the guest-ranch project. So the more money the rodeo makes, the more money we have for the guest ranch." He pulled his phone out of his pocket then looked at Piper. "Hey, I need to get back. You okay?"

"Yes, thanks for checking in on me. Wait a minute. I have something for you." She dug into her tote bag and pulled out a chain with a cross engraved on a silver medallion. She wrapped her fingers around it a moment, then pressed it into Bear's hand. "This is just a silly thing, but I'd given this necklace to Ry before his first rodeo and he wore it at every event. The night before he died, though, the chain had snapped. I'd picked up a new one, but didn't see him in time to give it to him before he rode. I don't believe in luck or anything. And I'm not superstitious to believe if he'd been wearing it, he would've been safe. But I want you to have it. You don't have to wear it. Put it in your pocket if you want to have a little piece of Ryland with you when you ride."

He opened his hand and lifted the silver chain. Sunlight glinted off the thick cross. He turned it over and read, "Psalm 28:7."

"'The Lord is my strength and my shield; my heart trusted in him, and I am helped: therefore my heart greatly rejoiceth; and with my song will I praise him.' Ryland recited it every morning before he rode."

A muscle jumped in the side of Bear's clenched jaw as he swallowed again. He rubbed a thumb and forefinger over his eyes, then brushed them on his jeans. He cupped Piper's chin, kissed her lightly then touched his forehead to hers. "Thank you, Piper. This means more than you'll ever know."

His voice, deep and throaty, sent a fresh rush of tears to her eyes. She tried to blink them back, but one trailed down her cheek.

He thumbed it away and blew out another breath. "I really need to get back. Will you stay? For me, too?"

She looked at the rough fingers touching her skin, then faced the man who held her close. She gave him a single nod, not trusting her voice. He grinned, kissed her again then jogged down the bleachers.

Piper settled her sunglasses in place and

watched him walk away. Instead of feeling that same sense of fear, though, tentative peace settled in her bones as she recited Psalm 28:7 over in her head.

After she and Ryland had got married, they started attending church, gave their hearts to the Lord then did their best to lead godly lives. But after his death, she turned away from those promises.

Did she really believe the Lord was her strength? If so, then why had she been trying to go it alone for so many years?

She continued to ponder that even ninety minutes after the stands had been filled to standing-room only. The Stone family crowded together, munching on hot dogs, popcorn and cotton candy. They included her in their conversations as if she were one of them. They cheered just as loudly for Avery as they had for Tanner during the mutton bustin' and the stick horse races.

As the bull-riding event loomed, Piper's insides tightened.

"And now, returning to the arena, legendary rider Bear Stone has entered the pen. Through the draw, he'll be riding Daredevil." The judge's voice echoed across the countryside.

Piper felt the color drain from her face

as a chill swept through her. Heart racing, she whipped around and looked up at Cole. "What? Did he say Daredevil? The one that killed Ryland? Why is that bull still on the circuit?"

Shaking his head and his mouth grim, Cole gripped her shoulder. "I don't know, Piper."

Piper wanted to push her way through the crowd, rush over to the pen and demand Bear get off the dangerous animal. But she couldn't move. Her body tensed and she fisted her hands as he climbed on top of the animal in the bucking chute, wearing the required padded vest, leather chaps and helmet.

Time slowed as he wrapped the tail—the end of the bull rope—around his left hand. He gave a curt nod, and the chute gate swung open.

The black-as-night bull stormed into the arena, spinning and bucking, his back legs flying off the ground. Bear jerked, then leaned and weaved with the movements of the raging animal, his right hand high in the air. As he was thrust forward, Daredevil's head came up, catching Bear in the shoulder with one of his horns.

The crowd gasped. Piper's fist flew to her mouth. Her throat burned as bile rose from her stomach. She covered her face. She couldn't breathe. She couldn't watch.

The timer raced as seconds felt like hours. Around her, the sea of voices sounded as if they were under water.

She closed her eyes and the image of Ryland's still body lying in the arena dirt flashed in her mind.

The buzzer sounded, and her eyes flew open as Bear's family jumped to their feet, arms in the air, screaming and clapping.

But Piper froze, unable to take her gaze off the man as he nearly somersaulted off the animal's back.

He jumped to his feet as the bullfighters, dressed in their red shirts, jeans and protective gear, drew the bull's attention away from him. Bear scrambled up and over the fence as the judges' scores flashed on the screen.

Piper released the breath she'd been holding.

"First place! Did you see that? Talk about a comeback," Wyatt shouted behind her.

Despite the warm evening, she shivered as ice slid through her veins. Tears rushed to her eyes as she pushed to her feet.

Two things became abundantly clear— Bear was born to ride. The graceful way he moved with the animal was like watching some sort of athletic ballet. And she wouldn't stand in his way. She couldn't be the one to keep him from doing what he obviously loves.

But she couldn't watch another performance like that again and wonder if he'd walk away with more than an injured shoulder…or even walk away at all.

This would be her last rodeo. That meant moving on with her life without Bear.

Chapter Thirteen

The Stone family deserved to celebrate. Bear earned that victory.

But Piper couldn't stay.

She needed to escape to the security of her home before anyone noticed her missing.

With Avery spending the night with her grandparents, Piper wasn't thrilled about going home to an empty house, but it was better than staying where memories threatened to suffocate her.

"Piper, wait up!"

She closed her eyes, exhaled and contemplated pretending not to hear Bear's request, but he'd see through that in half a second. Knowing him, he wouldn't stop until he got what he wanted.

He reached for her arm and turned her toward him. "Hey, where are you going?"

"Home." She lowered her gaze. She

couldn't look at him. Couldn't be drawn to him. Not if she needed to put necessary distance between them.

"Why?"

"Because that's where I live. For now."

"Funny girl."

"I wasn't trying to be funny."

"I meant why aren't you celebrating with the rest of the family?" He jerked his thumb toward the stands.

"They're your family, Bear. This is your celebration. Not mine." Even as she voiced the words, her throat thickened and tears burned her eyes.

Why did it feel like goodbye?

"We could change that, you know?" Low and throaty, his voice traveled over her, warming those places that felt numb by the events she'd just witnessed.

Despite her best attempts, she looked up at him and kicked herself for being weak. "Planning to ask your parents to adopt me?"

He laughed, the sound an arrow to her chest. "Not likely. Three sisters are plenty." He stepped closer and slid his arms around her waist, drawing her to him. He smelled of heat and sweat and victory. "I had another role in mind."

No need to pretend she didn't know what

he was talking about. He'd hinted at it a couple of weeks ago at the ranch house. The way his face softened and his eyes shone caused her breath to catch in her chest.

Another time, another place, maybe she'd be throwing her arms around his neck and making promises she was more than ready to keep.

She grasped his elbows and gently released herself from his embrace. "No, Bear. It wouldn't work."

"Piper, I've loved you since high school when the three of us hung out together. When you and Ry got together, I shoved those feelings in a box and stayed out of your way. You asked why I'm still single. That's because I've lost my heart only once. This isn't the place I'd expected but the timing couldn't be more perfect. I love you, Piper. I want you to be my wife, and I want Avery as my daughter."

"Bear." She couldn't say more than to utter his name. She bit her lip as tears pounded her eyes.

More than anything she wanted to give in to the longings of her heart. To step back into the circle of his love and say yes. But she couldn't. She took a step back, gently moving away from him, and shook her head. "I can't."

"Can't or won't?" The pain in his voice created a hole in her chest.

"Is there a difference?"

"If you tell me you don't love me and there will never be anything more between us, then I will take you at your word. But if you're saying no out of fear, then I'm not going anywhere. We belong together, Piper."

"We want different things." She waved a hand toward the arena. "You were magnificent out there. The way you held on after getting hooked in the shoulder. Then that dismount was the envy of every gymnast."

The side of his mouth slid up. "That was purely accidental."

"Accident or not, it made for a great show. You deserve the buckle, Bear. And many more buckles. Riding is in your blood, but I can't watch you event after event, wondering when I am going to lose you."

"Not every bull rider ends up like Ryland."

Piper tapped her head, her eyes pooling with tears. She blinked them back. "I know that in here." She palmed a hand over her chest. "But here...well, I can't reconcile my heart with my head."

"If I give up riding, then you'll say yes?"

"No, because you wouldn't be giving it up for the right reasons. You'd come to resent me for it."

"You don't know that." He released her and

took a step back, shaking his head. "I just can't win with you, can I?"

"It's not about winning. It's about protecting Avery. And me."

"There's a difference between protecting and being fearful, Piper. Make sure you're not confusing one with the other."

"I'm not confused about what I want. Everything I do is for my daughter and her future. To give her a life of security. Avery's been accepted into Centennial Academy. As soon as I come up with the rest of the tuition, I'll be looking for an apartment in Durango. You were born to be a cowboy. Are you ready to give that up and move to the city?" She pulled out of his grasp and walked away, trying to hold it together until she could find solace in the privacy of her vehicle.

"I'd move mountains to be with you, if you'd give me the chance to prove it. You want security for Avery, but I know you want that for yourself, too. I can give that to you... to both of you. But before you make these plans for your daughter, be sure you take time to ask what she wants, too." His voice rose as he called after her.

"Barrett Stone, how does it feel to be the Comeback Cowboy?" A woman with long dark hair and dressed in black approached them. She thrust a microphone in his face as a large man with a news camera followed behind her.

Piper stopped and closed her eyes as heat seared her cheeks. How much had they heard?

"Hey, guys. I'm not a comeback anything. Just a guy who stayed on a bull for eight seconds. Now if you'll excuse me—"

"Did you just propose to Piper Healy? Isn't she your best friend's widow? How does it feel to be back in the arena five years after Ryland Healy lost his life? Where are you going from here?"

Piper tightened her grip on her tote bag and headed to her car. She wasn't about to wait around for Bear's responses.

Comeback Cowboy.

Perfect name for him. He deserved his moment in the limelight. But she didn't want to be any part of it. She preferred her safe life in the shadows. She had Avery to think of. And she refused to allow her daughter to get hurt by rehashing the past.

Ryland was gone. Why couldn't they leave the past where it belonged and move on to something else?

"Hey, hey, pretty lady, where are you running off to?" Chet McNeil stepped out of the darkness and towered over her, his boozy breath clouding around her.

"Out of my way, Chet. I'm going home." She tried to move around him, but he blocked her escape.

He reached for her arm and dug his fingers into the skin below her elbow. "I saw you give Stone the brush-off."

"Let go of me." She yanked her arm out of his grasp, wincing as his polished nails sliced her skin. Her heart picked up speed but she refused to cower under his menacing height. The man was nothing more than a bully. She pushed past him and jogged toward the ranch house, wishing she had a little more than the moonlight to guide her.

Heavy steps stumbled behind her. Chet caught her shoulder, his fingers digging into the collar of her dress, and forced her to turn. "Don't you walk away from me, you little—"

"Let go of her, McNeil."

At the menacing growl in Bear's voice, Piper swallowed the whimper that nearly spilled past her lips and forced her knees not to buckle.

He released her so quickly that she would've stumbled if Bear hadn't rushed behind and caught her. His arms tightened around her.

"You're safe, Piper. No one's going to hurt you again."

"What're you gonna do about it, Cowboy? Take another swing at me?" McNeil's words slurred as he staggered toward them.

Bear moved in front of Piper, his palm up to stop Chet. "I nearly lost my career over you once. I'm not stupid enough to make the same mistake twice. I will talk Piper into pressing charges against you for assault."

Chet scoffed. "It's her word against mine. Who's going to believe her?"

"I will."

"No one will believe anything you say. A few chosen words to my dad, and your career will be toast before it gets started again."

"We'll believe her."

McNeil whipped around to find Wyatt, Cole and Deacon standing behind him. Along with the long-haired reporter and her crew, who continued to film the entire debacle.

He threw his hands up. "Hey, now. She came on to me."

She stepped around Bear, tears burning her eyes. "That's a lie. You accosted me as I was leaving the field."

"Prove it, you—"

"Choose your words carefully, Chet." Deacon stood between the men.

"You Stones always stick together," he sneered.

Deacon nodded. "Pretty much. That's what family does."

"Whatever. I'm outta here. She's not worth it."

"Not so fast, McNeil." An officer from the Aspen Ridge Police Department pulled a pair of handcuffs from his gear belt. "You can talk at the station."

McNeil protested with more name-calling as the officer cuffed him, spoke to him in a tone she couldn't hear and led him back to the field where his patrol vehicle was parked.

With her face scorned from shame and her arm and shoulder aching against Chet's roughness, Piper wanted nothing more than to escape back to her apartment, crawl into bed and wish she could turn back time to where she never set foot at the rodeo.

Attending had been a mistake. In a town as small as Aspen Ridge, there was no way to protect her daughter this time from the gossip that would be spreading within minutes.

Why hadn't she just stayed home?

It wasn't supposed to happen this way.

Bear wanted to wad the weekend paper into a ball, throw it in the fireplace and strike a match. But that wouldn't be enough to burn away the gossip being stirred by the headlines that managed to make national news.

He'd been an idiot to blurt out the proposal to Piper in the open like that, then keep running his mouth when it was clear she wanted nothing to do with him. To have the reporter catch it all on film and dog him for an interview…well, that was just perfect.

What had he been thinking? Piper deserved better.

Much better than him.

Seeing her in the stands gave him the confidence he needed to climb into the chute and onto the angry animal's back.

Five years ago, adrenaline sluicing through his veins drove him to ride as much as he could. To score the points. To hear his name being called. To win the buckles. Gripping the tail of the bull rope and feeling the angry animal dance beneath him fueled the excitement as the crowd watched and waited and cheered. All to make his family proud.

But last night was different.

He wanted to ride. To prove he deserved to be back in the arena where he belonged. But the moment he made contact with the bull, Ryland's lifeless body flashed through his mind. He had to talk himself into completing the ride. To prove he wasn't going to allow any deep-seated fears get in the way of his dream.

Except it didn't feel like his dream to nod and have the chute gates fly open.

While he held tight and moved with the bucking animal, he'd questioned his choices as his body jerked and heaved. Was that really what he wanted to do with his life? Travel the circuit and spend so much time away from those he loved?

Once the buzzer screamed and Daredevil finally flung him off his back, Bear had scrambled over the fence with his heart in his throat. Breathing heavily and wincing at the pain in his shoulder, he searched the stands for Piper, but he couldn't find her hidden behind his family jumping and cheering for him. Once she finally stood, the look on her face iced his blood.

She was the first person he wanted to share in his victory. Instead of hanging out with his family, she had disappeared into the crowd. He'd wanted nothing more than to find her.

The judges commented on his ride and the bull's movements. Once they released their scores, shooting him to first place, the crowd roared and chanted his name.

He should've been thrilled. Taking first

place and winning that buckle gave him the career recognition he thought he had wanted.

But without Piper by his side, being a bull rider lost its appeal. He wanted her and everything that came with building a life with her and Avery.

Thanks to that stupid newspaper article, he was about to lose everything all over again.

Comeback Cowboy or Casanova Cowboy?

The grainy black-and-white picture showed Bear's hand in McNeil's face while he kept a hand on Piper's arm. Once again, Bear looked like the poster child for an anger-management class. Anyone who witnessed what had happened could attest to the truth.

But the public didn't care about facts. They based their opinions on speculation and other peoples' comments.

Bear tossed the paper on the coffee table and moved to the kitchen to refill his cup. He needed to head back to the ranch and get started on chores. At least he could escape on Ranger, his bay paint, and head to the fields where nosy reporters, pushy cameramen and obnoxious star-seeking cowboys weren't allowed.

A quick knock on his front door sounded. His heart jammed in his throat. Piper?

He hurried across the hardwood floor in

his bare feet, pulled it open and forced his expression to remain neutral, so his visitors didn't see his disappointment.

Eugene stood on his front porch next to a woman a little older than Bear's mother.

Bear stepped back and held the door open wider. "Eugene, good morning. Come in."

Eugene moved aside and allowed the woman dressed in studded jeans, red boots and a matching red leather jacket to pass by him. Her expensive perfume clouded around him.

Eugene touched the woman's arm and smiled. "Jess, this is Barrett Stone, but his friends and family call him Bear. Bear, this is my sister, Jessica Wylie."

"Wylie as in Wylie's Western Wear?" Bear hoped his voice didn't crack like a pubescent thirteen-year-old.

The woman with thick dark hair that fell in soft waves around her face and sparkling blue eyes shot him a warm smile as she extended her hand. "The one and the same. Although, the Wylie comes from my husband, Rod. He was called away on business. Nice to meet you, Barrett."

He shook her hand. "Nice to meet you, ma'am. Please come in." Bear led them into the open living room and waved a hand toward the dark brown leather sectional. "Have a seat. Would you like some coffee?"

Good thing he'd picked up his mess before reading the paper.

At their nods, he returned to the kitchen, filled two more cups, reached for the cream and sugar, then looked around for something to carry everything. Other than family, no one else visited, so he was lacking in hospitality.

After handing the coffee to his guests, he returned to the kitchen for spoons and cream and sugar. He tossed the newspaper into the basket next to the floor-to-ceiling stone fireplace, then set everything on the chunky square coffee table nicked from boot heels and coffee cup rings.

"I'm surprised you could find me." After refilling his own cup, he took a seat on the end of the sectional.

Eugene poured a little milk into his coffee and stirred. "We stopped at the ranch. Your folks directed us out here. Hope it's okay we dropped by unannounced."

"Yeah, sure. Not a problem. I'm just a little surprised, that's all."

Jessica sipped her coffee, then held it in the palm of her hand. "Actually, I'm the one who wanted to meet with you and asked Eugene to introduce us."

"Meet with me? Why?"

"I watched your performance last night, and I was quite impressed with what I saw. You handled that bull with care and moved well when he tried to throw you off his back. I've been a part of the rodeo circuit for decades. I've watched riders from around the world, but you really stood out to me."

Bear didn't know what to say to that. He rubbed a hand across his warm jaw. "Thank you, ma'am."

"Call me Jess." She reached into her leather purse, pulled out a small case, retrieved a card and handed it to him. "Wylie's Western Wear would like to sponsor you as you return to the riding circuit. Normally, I'd approach your agent, but I did some online research and couldn't find your site or your sports agency listed anywhere."

Heat climbed up his neck. Bear ran a thumb over the embossed logo of an upturned red horseshoe with three black *W*s wrapped around it on the textured business card. "Yeah, after my career bit the dust, my agency dropped me."

"Their loss, if you ask me. If you're interested in considering our company as a sponsor, we can schedule a time to review the contract and get you fitted for gear from our company. Then we'll do a photo shoot and make you the face of the Wylie's Western Wear brand."

Was this for real?

Bear studied the logo once again, then looked at her. "Why me?"

"Because you represent what we're looking for in our athletes. I know you had a rough go of it when you lost your career, but I've been talking with Eugene and listening to him list your attributes. We're a faith-based company, and we love redemption stories. We believe you have what it takes to carry our brand with honor and integrity."

With his elbows balanced on his knees, Bear dropped his gaze to the grains in the hardwood floor, blinking several times to clear his blurring vision. His throat thickened.

Somebody, other than his family, actually believed in him?

Now what?

He lifted his eyes and found Eugene and Jess watching him. "Jess, thank you for this opportunity. You have no idea what it means to me. Would you mind if I took some time to think about it?"

"I'd be disappointed if you didn't." Still holding her cup in her left hand, she stood and extended her right one. "Barrett, it's been a pleasure meeting you. My number and email are on the card. Feel free to reach out to me with any questions you have. I know it's a lot to take in. My family believes in you, and we feel you'll be a great asset to our team."

He shook her hand again. "Call me Bear. I'll think this through, talk to my family and get back in touch with you."

He walked them to the door. After they left, he closed it behind them and leaned against it. He scrubbed both hands over his face, then let out a whoop.

Finally.

Maybe just maybe his career had a chance for redemption. Less than an hour ago, he was ready to walk away. But now with this opportunity of having someone invest in him, how did he choose between his career and the woman he loved?

Chapter Fourteen

Piper couldn't wait to leave Aspen Ridge.

Maybe a fresh start could erase the humiliation of the past eighteen hours. After filing her report at the police station, she'd gone to her car, only to be subjected to a nosy reporter's inquisition. The local reporter's story had been picked up by national news, so people across the county had witnessed her embarrassment.

Now that she'd received Avery's acceptance letter, she could get the paperwork submitted along with the down payment and move forward with finding them a place to live in Durango. And shake the dust of Aspen Ridge off her feet. Or at least as her residence.

She planned to turn the homes she cleaned over to other members of her team and expand her business in the Durango area. Sure, the competition would be tougher, but hopefully her recommendations would speak for themselves.

But for now, she needed to get to work. Maybe scrubbing walls and mopping floors would take her mind off this past weekend's disaster.

Doubtful, but it was worth a try.

She gathered her purse, keys and to-go mug of coffee and headed to the door. She opened it and found Bear standing on her front steps, fist poised to knock.

The sight of him sent her heart slamming against her rib cage. But she forced her feelings aside and schooled her tone. "Bear. What are you doing here?"

"Good morning to you, too. Got a minute?"

"Actually, I'm on my way to work. Can this wait?"

"Just five minutes, I promise."

She glanced at her watch and felt her resolve slipping. Sighing, she stepped back and let him pass by her. "Okay, five minutes. Come in."

He moved past her, smelling of soap and coffee. She set her things on the side table next to the door, then crossed her arms over her chest. "What's up?"

Bear stuffed a hand in his front pocket, then scratched the back of his head. "I had a chat with Eugene and his sister. You know her?"

"Jess? I met her a few years ago at one of Eugene's picnics."

"So you know she owns Wylie's Western Wear?"

"Yes, along with her husband. She's asked if Avery could model some of their clothes, but I declined. I didn't want that life for her."

"She said if I returned to the bull-riding circuit, they'd love to sponsor me."

Do not react.

"I see. What did you tell her?"

"I wanted to think it over. Talk about it with my family. And you."

"Me? You know how I feel. Do you really think I'm going to change my mind? Especially after being humiliated on national news over what happened last night?"

He cupped a hand over his eyes, then dropped it. "I know. And I'm so sorry about that. I tried calling."

"I didn't want to talk." She lowered her gaze, not wanting to get caught in the pull she felt when staring into his eyes.

"To anyone or just me?"

"Bear, there's nothing else to say. You know where I stand."

And it couldn't be by his side, where she knew he wanted her to be.

"Piper, look at me. Please."

His low tones with a touch of pleading fraying the edges nearly had her vaulting into his arms. But she forced herself to remain where she stood because one step toward him could quickly change her mind, and her heart couldn't afford another loss.

But she did as he asked and lifted her eyes to meet his leaf green ones.

He took a step toward her and reached for her hands. His rough, weathered skin felt warm against hers. "Do you love me?"

"What does that have to do with anything?"

He laughed. "It has everything to do with anything."

"Bear, don't do this, please. I have a busy day and don't have time right now to discuss this."

"Okay, fine. When then?"

"When then what?"

"When can we discuss it?"

"We want different things. I just don't see us working out."

"If you love me, then everything else will fall into place."

"Even if it means leaving the rodeo career

you want to redeem and the ranch you love so much?"

"The ranch? Why would I have to leave that?"

Piper pulled her hands from his and reached into her purse. She pulled out an envelope and handed it to him. "Like I told you last night—Avery's been accepted into the Centennial Academy. We're moving to Durango after Christmas. Are you ready to head to the city?"

He took the envelope but didn't read it. Then he looked at her. The light in his eyes dimmed as lines deepened around his mouth. "This will be a great opportunity for Avery. Was she excited when you told her?"

Heat warmed her cheeks. "I haven't told her yet. I wanted to be sure she could get in before we talked about it."

"Piper—"

She held up a hand. "Don't. I don't need anyone else criticizing my parenting skills. I'm going to talk to her, and we'll visit the school together. She'll see the wonderful new opportunities in store for her."

"And when she asks about her friends, her rodeo camp, her Nana and Pappy?"

"She will make new friends, and she will

still have her weekends with her grandparents, so that won't be an issue."

He handed the envelope back to her. "Of course, I want what's best for her, too. Thanks for telling me."

The clock on the wall chimed at the top of the hour. "Listen, I really need to get to work. Can we talk more about this later?"

Bear lifted his hands, then dropped them at his sides. "Yeah, sure. Whatever. Is there anything to talk about if you're making all of these plans without me? I learned about this sponsorship, and you were the first person I wanted to share it with. But you've had that letter for a few days now and last night was the first I heard about it."

"Two days, actually. I got it the day after our ride. But you knew I was doing this."

"You're right, I did. My point is you don't trust me to be a part of your life, and I don't think you ever will. You say I'm not the same person you knew years ago, but in your heart, there's no room for me. Goodbye, Piper." He opened the door quietly, slipped out and closed it behind him.

Why did his last two parting words sound so final?

She dropped the envelope on the table next to her purse and pressed her fist against her mouth as her throat thickened and tears flooded her eyes.

After pulling in a couple of deep breaths to staunch the emotions pummeling her chest, she grabbed her purse, headed outside, locking the door behind her.

She tossed her purse on the passenger seat and reached for her seat belt. She dropped her phone in the cup holder and realized she'd left her coffee inside. She slammed the heel of her hand against the steering wheel.

As she drove past the diner, she pulled into an empty spot near the rear. Grabbing her purse, she exited the vehicle, and headed inside.

Scents of bacon, pancakes and fresh coffee lingered in the air. Any other time her mouth would be watering, but today, the smells made her stomach turn.

She headed for the counter as Lynetta came out of the kitchen carrying two pies. "Hey, sugar, I'll be with you in a minute."

Her warm smile arrowed its way to Piper's aching heart.

Lynetta.

In all of her thoughts about moving to Durango, she'd forgotten about the woman who was one of her closest friends. Her truthteller. Her confidante. How would she cope in the city without her daily drop-ins at the diner?

Well, she'd have to learn to deal with it. Avery would be making some changes, and so would she. Durango was only a forty-five-minute drive. It wasn't like she wouldn't see Lynetta and Pete again.

As she waited for Lynetta to finish placing the pies in the bakery case, Piper scanned the counter, and her eyes caught sight of a flyer advertising the Stones' guest ranch.

Now was the best time to let her friend know her intentions so they could get someone else to finish the project.

"Okay, hon. What can I get you?" Lynetta wiped her hands on a dish towel, then reached for a paper to-go cup. She filled it with coffee and slid it in front of Piper.

Piper looked down at the rich brew awaiting her cream and stared at her reflection. Her eyes burned once again.

Lynetta touched her cheek. "Hey, are you okay?"

Biting her bottom lip, Piper shook her head. Then she looked up at her friend. "I need to go back on my word."

Lynetta frowned. "Your word? About what?"

"The guest-ranch project. I can't complete it. I'll give you detailed notes for the next person who steps in to finish once the cabins are ready to be built."

"What's going on?"

The compassion in her friend's voice pushed through the dam of emotions pressing against Piper's chest. Standing at the counter in a diner full of people, she covered her face with her hands and sobbed, adding to her humiliation.

Lynetta rounded the corner and wrapped Piper into her embrace. She steered her through the swinging door that led into the kitchen and to her office.

In the tiny room, Lynetta moved a stack of papers off a chair and pointed for Piper to sit. Then she handed her a box of tissues. Lynetta sat in the office chair and spun toward Piper. She leaned forward and grabbed her hands. "Tell me what's going on."

As if her words had a voice of their own, she spilled about the rodeo, the chaos afterward, Avery's acceptance into the new school, and Bear. The more she spoke, the more she realized just what a mess her life was. And she had no idea how to begin cleaning it up.

Why had he expected anything different from Piper?

She'd made her feelings very clear last

night and again this morning with her plans to leave. Apparently, he was a glutton for punishment.

Maybe a part of him had hoped the sponsorship would help change her mind. But wearing someone's logo on his chest didn't protect him against the danger of being hooked again. Or worse.

As he parked his Jeep in front of the ranch house, his phone rang. He glanced at the number and didn't recognize it. For half a second, he considered letting it go to voice mail, but when it rang again, he answered, "Barrett Stone."

"Hey, Barrett. It's Dalton McNeil. We'd like to have a sit-down with you at your earliest convenience."

Bear's gut tightened. "About what?"

"Well, I don't want to get into it over the phone. The council wants to address a few things."

"I can be there in fifteen minutes." Might as well get it over with.

"Sounds good. See you then." The line went silent.

Bear gripped the steering wheel, then blew out a breath.

Most likely Chet had run to his daddy, and now Bear was about to pay the price.

He glanced down at his clean jeans and red T-shirt. Good enough. He wasn't about to dress to impress, especially if they were going to give him the boot over something Chet may have claimed he did.

Fifteen minutes later, he parked his Jeep in front of the council building and headed inside the office that smelled of lemon oil and pipe tobacco.

Removing his hat and smoothing down his hair, he nodded to Wanda, the receptionist. "Morning, ma'am."

"Morning, Bear." She smiled and pointed to the open door to the conference room. "They're waiting for you."

"Thank you." Drawing in a deep breath, he let it out slowly and flexed his fingers. He stepped inside to find Dalton, Beau, Rex and Victor sitting on one side of the heavy oak table. A single chair sat empty across from them.

"Morning, gentlemen." He reached across the table and shook their hands.

Dalton gestured to the empty chair. "Have a seat."

He sat, placed his hat on his knee and folded his hands on the table. He looked at each of the men. Dalton, Beau and Rex stared at him as if he'd come in covered in manure.

But Victor had compassion in his eyes. His mentor had always been his ally. Hopefully, that bode well for him during this meeting. "So, what can I do for you?"

Dalton opened a leather padfolio and pulled out a folded newspaper. He slid it across the table. "For starters, you can explain this."

Bear clenched his jaw. Just as he figured. He didn't even pick up the paper. Instead, he leaned back in the chair. "What would you like to know?"

"The council's a bit concerned about the events that transpired after the rodeo. Looks like history repeated itself once again."

"How do you figure?"

"Laying a hand on my boy, for starters."

"You can't be serious. I didn't touch him."

"The picture on the front page says differently." Dalton leaned forward, looked at the other men then nodded. "We take allegations like this quite seriously."

"What allegations?"

"We have it on good authority you struck Chet McNeil after the rodeo."

"Well, your authority is wrong. I didn't lay a hand on that jerk except to keep him away from Piper Healy."

"Hey, now. That's my son you're talking about."

"I'm well aware. And your son has been charged with assault. Yet you're going after me."

"Well, now, that was a little misunderstanding between my boy and that little lady."

Bear pushed to his feet, knocking his chair sideways, and leaned forward, palms pressed against the table. "He left bruises. That's not a misunderstanding. That's assault. I tried to stop him from hurting her any further. There are witnesses to back up my story."

"Witnesses?" Dalton pulled out another sheet of paper from his padfolio. "Looks like those witnesses are family members. Am I right?"

"My family saw what happened, yes. Plus, the reporter and her cameraman who filmed what was going on."

"So, of course, they're going to side with you."

"Just as you're siding with your son's lies and accusations. Once again, he's in the wrong and I'm getting blamed."

Rex lifted a beefy hand covered in calluses. "Simmer down, young man. We're just trying to get to the bottom of what happened."

"You guys have formed an opinion about what happened already. Nothing I say is going to change that. What about the reporter and cameraman who filmed what was going on? Have you talked to them?"

Dalton pointed to the paper. "Kind of speaks for itself, doesn't it? There's no mention of my boy hurting anyone."

"You may want to talk to the officer who took him to the station."

"That's been cleared up. Like I said—a misunderstanding."

Bear shook his head and scrubbed a hand over his face. "I don't believe this. Your son breaks the law and it's a misunderstanding. I defend a lady's honor and I get called on the carpet."

Dalton cleared his throat and folded his hands in front of him. "In light of recent events, we voted and decided it would be best to put your membership on hold for the time being until this little mess is cleared up."

Bear opened his mouth but the words stuck in his throat. A punch in the face would've hurt less. He turned away from the table, righted the chair and picked up his hat. As he ran his fingers along the brim, he looked at three of the men who had condemned him before hearing his story. Then he turned his attention to Victor. "Do you believe me?"

"Yes, son, I do. I voted against this whole charade." He waved his hand over the table.

Bear nodded and held out a fist to his mentor and friend. "Thanks, man."

Victor bumped his fist. "You got it."

Then Bear turned to the other men. "Keep my card. I don't want it, and I don't need to be a part of a corrupt organization that allows such unacceptable behavior against women to go unchallenged. Yet you've already voted against me without getting facts and hearing my side of the story. Again." He settled his hat in place. "I'm out."

As he exited the building, the anger and hurt simmering in his stomach twisted his gut. He'd expected fallout from that incident, but not once had he considered his association membership being on the line. Without that membership card, he couldn't participate in any of their sponsored rodeo events. Once she heard of the council's decision, Jess Wylie would be pulling her offer, anyway.

Chet McNeil's threats to ruin his career came to fruition. While Bear still stood by his choices to deck the jerk five years ago and defend Piper from the creep's unwanted advances last night, the shame of what happened washed over him. He would always be a disgraced cowboy defined by his past mistakes.

Chapter Fifteen

Piper needed to pull herself together.

The more she tried to stop the tears from flowing, the harder they came. And Lynetta had a dining room full of customers to tend to. She didn't need to be babysitting a hot mess in her office.

"I'm sorry."

"For what, sugar? You've done nothing wrong." She cupped Piper's chin. "You're hurting, and ole Lynetta has been blessed with big shoulders to cry on."

"I'm going to miss you when we move to Durango."

"Honey, I'm not going anywhere. Besides, Pete and I head into the city quite often these days to help his sister and nephew as he recovers from surgery."

"How's he doing?"

"Good. Good. The doctors are pleased with

his progress and think he can be back to work in a couple of months."

"That's great to hear. So he's planning to move forward on constructing the cabins."

"Yes, if we still go with that route."

"You're thinking differently now?"

"Well, not so much differently, but the yurts have been a success. With the soft launch, we're booked all the way into the upcoming year. Pete and I met with Deac and Nora. We're thinking of expanding and getting more put up before the snow begins to fall. With WinterFest coming up, we can offer accommodations for out-of-town travelers who want to spend more than a day in the area. Macey's been working up some numbers lately and Wyatt's been mapping out some trails for sleigh rides and things like that."

"See? You guys don't need me, after all." She tried not to feel like she was being replaced already, but this was the family's business…and she was not a part of that family.

"We will always need you. In fact, I don't accept your resignation. You gave me your word, and I want you to see it through. You're not alone in this, and I don't want you to back out because you're afraid."

"Afraid? I quit because I'm going to be moving."

"When I asked you to take on this project, I said you've got grit, and I still believe that. You're not moving for another few months, at least. You quit now because of Barrett, and don't you deny it."

She couldn't lie to her friend any more than she could lie to herself. Lynetta was right. Piper wanted to quit because of Bear. Every time she was around him, he took down another chunk of the wall around her heart, leaving her exposed and vulnerable. How was she supposed to protect herself?

"You've come so far in your life. With God's help and grace, you can continue learning and growing, especially through these tough seasons. My mom always said, *'It may not be a good day, but there's always good in the day.'* And God is always good."

"I don't have a faith like yours. I haven't done enough good to earn God's love."

"Earn it? Child, God loves you unconditionally and freely. He doesn't love based on a merit system. He loved us so much He sent His own Son to the cross. If that's not unconditional love, then I don't know what is. You and I can't do enough to earn His love. That's the beauty of grace—He gives it freely."

"I've heard it so often in church, but I don't

feel it in here." Piper pressed a hand against her heart.

"That's the enemy getting a foothold in your thoughts, my dear. God sees you. He knows your every thought, your every sin, and yet, He loves and values you for who you are. Not for what you do. May I ask you a question?"

Piper lifted a shoulder. "Yeah, I guess."

"What do you truly want?"

"What do you mean?"

"What's your heart's desire?"

"I want to be loved and accepted for who I am. I want to be with someone who can give me the emotional security I need and not walk away when I make a mistake." Even as she spoke the words aloud, another chunk of the wall around her heart fell away. She raised her eyes and met Lynetta's warm ones shimmering with her own tears. "I've never said that to another person before."

"Right away, two men come to mind—God and my nephew. So now you need to make a choice—what are you going to do about it?"

Piper lowered her gaze to the shredded tissue in her lap. "Bear and I… That won't ever work."

"Why not?"

"We want different things. He loves bull riding, and that terrifies me. He loves his cabin and the ranch, and I'm moving to Durango."

"But he loves you more. I can see it every time he's around you. If he had to choose, I know my nephew well enough to know he'd choose you."

"And he'd come to resent me for that choice."

Lynetta clucked her tongue. "I don't think so."

"Ryland did."

"What?"

"I never told anyone, but after his first injury, I asked Ryland to stop riding. I was so afraid he was going to get hurt. He got mad and told me not to ask him to choose because I might not like his decision. I'm not going to make the same mistake with Bear—he knows how I feel about bull riding, but I'm not standing in his way. He needs to make his own choice."

"What if he has?"

"I told you about Jess Wylie's offer and he's pretty excited about it. That makes me think he wants to ride again."

"I loved your husband like he was one of my own, and I'm so sorry he lost his life so young. He had his priorities mixed up. He was drawn to the fame instead of putting you and Avery first."

"I can't change it."

"No, but you can't allow your fears to take hold and prevent you from having the life you deserve."

"What are you saying?"

"Fight for what you want, even if it means facing the fear that holds you back from giving your heart away a second time. I'm not so sure Bear's career is the real issue here."

"Then what is?"

"I think you're afraid of losing him and being alone again. Sure, bull riding is a dangerous sport, but most of the riders are well trained and responsible. My parents spent their entire lives on the ranch, which has its own dangers. But their lives were taken by a drunk driver who made an irresponsible, life-altering choice. If Bear goes back to bull riding, there is a risk he could get hurt...or worse. But he could also lose his life in another way, too. We can't cloak ourselves in fear for what may or may not happen. We need to punch those fears in the nose and lean into God so our faith in Him gives us the strength to live our best lives with those we love."

The image of Lynetta punching anything in the nose made Piper giggle. She wiped her eyes and reached for her friend. "You're a wise woman, Lynetta, and a good friend."

Lynetta stood, taking Piper with her, and

pressed a kiss to the top of her head. "I've had to fight through my own fears, sugar. But I couldn't do it with my own strength. I had to lean into the Lord and on Pete to see me through the years of infertility, losing my parents and learning how to run this diner on our own while grieving. You're a strong woman, Piper, and you're setting a great example for your daughter, but you don't have to go through life relying on yourself. Surrender those fears and allow God to work in your heart. Then He will help you to achieve your heart's desire, whatever that may look like."

Lynetta was right.

Every word.

Problem was Piper didn't know where to start.

For the first time in his life, Bear didn't want to go home.

He didn't want to face his family and let them see what a disgrace he was once again to the Stone name. He didn't want to see the disappointment in his father's face when he learned what a failure his son was…in life and in love.

And now the rodeo wasn't standing between him and Piper, and she was leaving. Maybe they just weren't meant to be together and he'd been chasing a pipe dream all these years.

As if steering on its own, his Jeep turned down the road that took him to Eugene's farm and apiary. He parked in the semicircular drive and found the man sitting in a rocking chair on the wide covered porch.

As Bear exited his truck, Eugene stood, leaning on his cane, and lifted a hand. "Morning, Barrett."

Bear removed his hat and climbed the steps. He extended his hand. "Hello again, sir. I hope you don't mind me dropping in like this."

"No. No. Not at all. I'm always up for company. Once Jess and Rod leave this afternoon, the house will be quiet again." He gestured to the matching hickory rocker. "Have a seat. Or maybe you're here to talk with my sister and want to head inside? Planning your big comeback to the rodeo circuit?"

"No, that's no longer an option." Shaking his head, Bear took a seat and kept his gaze focused on his hat as he scoured his brain for the right words. "Your sister isn't going to like what I have to say, so I'm not ready to talk with her just yet."

"What's going on, if you don't mind me asking?"

Bear blew out a breath and rubbed his

thumb and forefinger over his tired eyes. Setting his hat on the porch floor, he leaned back in the rocker and told Eugene about the events that transpired at the council office.

"I don't get why Chet is considered a golden child, and I'm always going to be defined by my mistakes. The truth is there, but they refuse to see it. I'm telling you now, some other woman is going to get hurt unless someone stops Chet now."

"Hopefully, Piper's word will go a long way with making that happen."

"I don't know—Dalton seemed convinced that little misunderstanding had been taken care of."

"I've known Dalton for years, and that boy of his has always had his daddy in his pocket. No way to parent, but Dalton has no one to blame but himself and Chet for their mistakes. As for you, young man, your story doesn't end here."

"What do you mean?"

"Just because you can't ride with this organization doesn't mean your rodeo career is over, unless you want it to be. Your story doesn't end with your mistakes. God isn't finished with you yet. This season of testing will become your testimony if you allow yourself to give it over to the Lord."

"Funny you should say that… Before you and Jess dropped by the cabin this morning, I was even wondering if I wanted to reclaim my rodeo career after all. I don't know. When I climbed on the back of that bull, it felt different, almost foreign."

"Well, it had been five years. In the arena, at least."

"True, but I can't explain it—I thought it was what I really wanted, but now, I'm not so sure. I just want to make my family proud."

"Son, I've known your family a long time. Your grandfather was a good friend of mine. Losing him felt like losing a part of myself."

"That's how I felt after Ry was killed."

"So you get it."

"Unfortunately."

"Your family is prouder of you than you'll ever know. They stood by you when the media butchered you. They continue to stand by you even when ridiculous reporters create unimaginative headlines for sensationalist media. Your mistakes are not failures."

"What would you call them, then?"

"Opportunities for growth and learning. You have a strong work ethic and do what needs to be done. I admire your integrity. You stand for justice."

"I haven't looked at it that way."

"That's because your perspective is a little blindsided right now." Using his cane to steady him, Eugene pushed to his feet. "Let's head inside. It's nearly lunchtime, and I don't know about you, but this conversation has worked up an appetite."

Bear couldn't say the same. He held up a hand. "Thank you for the offer, sir, but I've taken up enough of your time."

"Nonsense. Come inside and talk with Jess. I'm sure you're going to want to hear what she has to say."

"I respectfully disagree, sir."

"Call me Eugene. I haven't been called sir since I left the army." He moved to the door and opened it, waiting for Bear to step inside.

Not wanting to be rude, Bear complied. He entered the farmhouse and took in the dark flooring coupled with off-white walls. He kicked off his shoes next to the others lining the runner inside the door. Eugene gestured for Bear to follow him into the kitchen.

Male voices boomed with laughter as they entered the brightly lit room. Delicious smells spiraled from a pot simmering on the stove.

"Bear! Nice to see you. Come in and join us." Jess slid out from her chair at the table and stood behind a gray-haired man built like an ox. "This is my husband, Rod, and of course, you know Victor."

Bear shook hands with Rod and didn't even try to contain his surprise at seeing Victor in Eugene's kitchen. Now, more than ever, Bear wished he'd turned down Eugene's invitation. "Hey, Victor. I'm surprised to see you. Again."

Victor clamped a hand on Rod's shoulder. "Rod and I go way back. He helped me get Lil Riders started until he met this pretty young thing and ditched me."

"And I don't regret it for a minute." Rod gave his wife's hand a squeeze.

"Bear, Vic tells me you've had a busy morning."

Bear took the seat she offered. "It's been a day, that's for sure."

"Maybe we can help improve it."

"How so?"

Victor leaned forward, elbows on the table and hands clasped. "Bear, I'm sorry for what happened. When Dalton called the emergency meeting, I was against it one hundred percent. I went along because I wanted you to have someone in your corner, someone who believed you over the lies Chet's been spreading around town. After you left, I gave my notice to the council, effective immediately."

"But you've been on the council for thirty years."

"Yes, but for the past ten, Dalton's been running it into the ground. I don't want to be a part of a dirty organization. I've filed a complaint with the top brass, and we'll see what happens. Knowing Jess and Rod were in town for another day or so, I decided to drop by. I told them what happened without giving specifics, and Jess had an idea that we'd like to run past you."

"What's that?"

Still standing behind her husband, Jess rested her hands on his shoulders. "I've been around the rodeo nearly my whole life. I left Colorado and headed to New York to pursue a career in fashion design. Little did I expect to meet a cowboy in Madison Square Garden. We started Wylie's Western Wear, and the rest is history. Except now, we want to diversify a little."

"In what way?"

"I've been talking with Eugene, Rod and now Victor about forming a new rodeo association. Vic was one of the founding members of the one you were a part of, so he knows how to get us started. We're looking for men of integrity to be a part of it, and we'd like you to join us."

"Me? I have no experience with being on a rodeo council."

"Maybe not, but you believe in justice and fairness. You wouldn't let another cowboy get railroaded the way Dalton and his men did to you."

"My name's not held in high regard in the rodeo world, especially after this past weekend. Dalton and his son will do what they can to blackball me. Chet's held a grudge against me since we were kids."

"Let them. Those who know you will know the truth and that's what matters. You can't control what others say about you, but you have complete control over your own actions. Be the bigger man."

"My dad says that all the time."

"He's a wise man."

Bear looked at Victor. "Despite what Chet said, I didn't touch him except to keep him away from Piper. He marked her arm and her shoulder. He's lucky I didn't hit him in the jaw a second time. He touches her again, and I won't walk away."

Victor nodded, his eyes affirming Bear's words. "I have a brother-in-law at the department, and Chet's not going to be able to buy his way out of it this time, especially since there have been other complaints filed against him. I can't prove it yet, but I think he's responsible for the fire at the arena."

"Why? What did he stand to gain?"

"Who knows what goes through that boy's thick head. He's a spoiled, self-centered jerk who thinks the world revolves around him. I don't believe for a second any of the lies he's told."

"Thanks, Victor. That means a lot."

"I've got your back, kid. And that's why we want you to be a part of this new venture."

Bear nodded and lowered his gaze as he swallowed past the boulder forming in his throat. "May I have time to think about it? To be honest, I'm in love with Piper Healy, and she wants nothing to do with the rodeo. If I have to choose between her and this endeavor, then she'll win, even if it means leaving Aspen Ridge."

Eugene leaned forward. "Have you told her that?"

"Not the leaving part."

"Then go get the girl, but keep your heart open to what God may be calling you to do."

Bear appreciated Eugene's advice and needed to rely on God more than ever now. Because he had a feeling Piper wasn't going to be as easy to convince that she's been the only one for him…and had been since high school.

Chapter Sixteen

Piper had heard the way to a man's heart was through his stomach, and she hoped that was still true because she was up to her elbows in cupcake batter.

When she'd pulled out her cookbook for chocolate cupcakes, she couldn't decide between regular chocolate, peanut butter chocolate or German chocolate, so she decided to make them all. And Avery was more than happy to help, especially after the meltdown she'd had about the new school and moving.

No matter how much Piper tried to hype up the new adventure, Avery was adamant about not going. She even threatened to move in with her nana, which did not sit well with Piper.

Dealing with Sheila was another matter altogether. Piper wasn't armored for that battle yet. To soothe her sobbing daughter, they put the idea on hold.

Piper spent most of the night thinking through her decision. When she received an email notification this morning of Avery's tuition being paid, Piper called the school about their error. But there was no mistake.

Someone had paid for Avery's tuition.

Most likely Lynetta again.

But that gave Piper a new problem—did she force her daughter to go to a school that would help her to excel or stay with what she knew so she could remain with her friends?

She'd worry about that later.

Right now, she needed to deliver three dozen cupcakes before she lost her nerve.

After loading the cupcakes in the back of her SUV, she headed toward the ranch. When she reached Bear's cabin, she didn't see his Jeep in its usual parking spot. Did she wait? Knock on his door to see if he was home, anyway?

She should've called. Or at least texted. But she wanted it to be a surprise.

She stepped out of her car and heard a bark. Dakota.

She followed the sound and ended up at the trail that would take her to the yurts. She still needed to limit access so visitors didn't end up in his backyard.

She found Bear's Jeep parked in one of the empty spaces in front of the first yurt. She knocked on the open door frame. "Hello?"

Bear rounded the corner shirtless with a worn leather tool belt fastened low on his hips. Her heart leaped to her throat and she turned away.

Get a grip.

She'd seen a guy without a shirt before.

Bear met her in the doorway, T-shirt back on, and his hair tousled. "Piper. Hey. What's going on?"

"I stopped by your cabin and didn't see your Jeep. I heard Dakota's bark and followed it to find you here."

"He must've heard you pull up."

"I'm sorry we haven't come up with a way to guard your privacy yet."

"No worries at all. May not be an issue soon, anyway."

"What do you mean?"

"I'll explain after you tell me why you were looking for me."

Now that she had his attention, all her rehearsed words flew out of her head. "I brought you something. Actually, I made you something."

His eyes widened. "You did? Why?"

"To tell you I'm sorry."

"Piper, you have nothing to apologize for."

"Are you busy? Can you take a break?"

"Yeah, sure. I was just taking care of a few little things in each of the yurts."

"Can we walk back to your cabin for a few minutes?"

Bear unbuckled his tool belt and slung it over the platform railing. He whistled for Dakota, who came running up from the lake, fur wet and a stick in his mouth. Then he waved a hand in front of Piper. "Lead the way."

They walked silently back to her car. She popped the lift gate with the remote on her key fob. As they drew closer, scents of sugar and chocolate enveloped them. Piper picked up one of the containers and handed it to Bear. "Here. These are for you."

He popped the lid and his face softened. "You made me cupcakes."

Not trusting her voice, she nodded, her eyes filling with tears.

"Why?"

"To say I'm sorry." Her voice choked on the last word.

"And I told you—you have nothing to apologize for."

"But I feel like I do. I allowed my fears

from the past to get in the way of my future...
with the man I love."

Bear's hands stilled on the container. He
closed the lid carefully and set it on top of
the other two containers. Reaching for Piper,
he drew her close and cradled her face in his
hands. "You love me?"

She nodded. "I pushed you away because
I was afraid of what would happen if you re-
claimed your bull-riding career. I didn't want
to lose you like I lost Ryland. Lynetta helped
me to see it wasn't the rodeo I was afraid of,
but the fear of loss itself. Everyone who was
supposed to love me left. My dad left while
my mom was still pregnant so I never knew
him. My mom left because I was such a disappointment. Ryland left through death. I was
afraid of giving my heart away again, only to
be abandoned."

He touched his forehead to hers. "Not everyone who loves you has left. I'm here. I've
always been here, and I always will be. No
matter what."

"Even if I leave Aspen Ridge?"

"Even if. But what's with the if? I thought
it was a done deal and you were moving after
Christmas?"

"Maybe." Piper told him about Avery's re-
action to the news and being torn between

staying and going, especially now that the tuition had been paid. "I asked Lynetta about it, and she denied it like she denied paying my college tuition. I've never known her to lie before so I don't know why she just won't fess up about this."

Bear wrapped his arms around Piper and drew her close. "She wasn't lying. My aunt doesn't do that."

"I don't get it, then. If she and Pete didn't pay it, then who... Oh." Piper's breath caught. She put her hands on Bear's elbows and stepped back. Her voice dropped to a whisper. "You. It was you who paid my tuition and paid for Avery to go to this school."

He didn't deny it and the color climbing his neck proved she was right. Why hadn't she seen it before?

"Bear. Why?"

"Because I told Ryland I would take care of you. I overheard you telling Lynetta about your plans to drop out and I didn't want that to happen. And you really wanted Avery in this new school. I wanted what was best for her, too."

"I will pay you back. Every penny."

"No!" His face tightened, then he relaxed. "This is why I didn't tell you. I didn't want you to feel obligated. It was a gift, free and clear."

"I don't know what else to say, especially since I was a jerk to you for years. Thank you."

"That's all I need to hear. I love you, Piper. I have for years. I'll do what it takes to make you happy, even if it means moving to Durango."

Knowing she needed to trust God now more than ever, Piper shook her head through a fresh sheen of tears and pulled in a deep breath. She let it out slowly and touched his face. "I'm so proud of the man you are and look forward to spending the rest of my life getting to know you even more. I fell in love with a guy who believed in the power of dreams. So much so that he'd pay for others to achieve their own dreams. You need to see this rodeo dream to the finish."

He shook his head. "That's not going to happen."

"Why not? What about Jess's offer of sponsorship?"

He told her about his meeting with the rodeo council and ending his membership.

"Bear, I'm so sorry. I feel like this is partly my fault."

"None of this is your fault. The blame lies with Chet McNeil. I learned recently other women have filed complaints against him, so you need to be strong and see yours through to the finish. I'll be with you every step of the way."

"I like the sound of that. What will you do now?"

"Consider a compromise. Would you be open to that?"

"I trust you and will stand beside whatever you decide."

"Whatever *we* decide."

"We. I like the sound of that." She lifted her face and brushed a kiss across his lips.

He pulled her close and deepened the kiss, leaving her breathless.

Yet she could finally breathe.

Really exhale, because for the first time in five years, she didn't have to go through life relying on herself.

With Bear by her side and God guiding their decisions, she had a peace she hadn't felt in years.

And it came by trusting Him and offering her heart to the one person she knew would treasure it for the rest of their lives.

Bear couldn't think of a time when he was happier. Not when he won his first buckle or even when he stayed on the bull for eight seconds after returning to the arena after a five-year absence.

After kissing Piper again, Bear forced himself to move away from her lips. He had a lifetime to kiss her and he'd make every moment count.

"So about this compromise..." Her words were muffled against his shirt.

"Yes, that."

Taking her hand, he led her to the front porch, and they sat on the swing he'd made with his dad.

"Your place is beautiful, by the way."

"Thanks. It's been a sanctuary. I'll give you a tour in a bit."

She snuggled against his side. "I'd like that."

With an arm wrapped around her, he shared his conversation with Eugene, then the one regarding the new rodeo council. "When I drew Daredevil's name before the rodeo started, I really struggled to climb into that chute. I kept reciting Psalm 28:7 and saying I was doing it for Ry. To give him the victory he was denied. But then after all the applause and celebrations, I realized I wasn't sure I wanted that anymore. I asked God for guidance, and that's when Jess made her offer. But without being in the association, I couldn't ride, so having a sponsor didn't matter. I went to Eugene's to get some advice, and that's when they presented this new offer. With your blessing, I'd love to be a part of this. I'll be around the rodeo, but I won't be on the backs of bulls."

"I told you already—I'll stand beside you. I will admit returning to the arena is hard. Even though they're lessening, I still have nightmares about losing Ry, but I've been working with a counselor to help overcome my fears." She smiled up at him.

"Eugene?" He stroked her cheek.

"He's a good friend, but I meet with a female colleague of his."

"He told me he was a counselor, and knowing your close relationship with him, I'd assumed you'd been talking to him."

"He's kind and nonjudgmental, but we decided I might be more open with a female. My counselor's name is Maggie, and she lost her husband, too, so she understands my grief."

"He cares about you and Avery like family."

"That's because we are family. I'm learning family isn't always formed through biology. Sometimes your best families come together through heart."

He grabbed her hand and held it against his

chest. "I couldn't have said it better myself. I love you and I love Avery. I'd love for us to be a family someday."

"I'd like that, too." The love shining in her eyes had him kissing her again.

He curled her in the curve of his embrace. "There's something else I'd like you to consider."

"Sure, what's up?"

"I've been thinking about Eugene's Hives for Healing program. I find it kind of fascinating. Then I had a conversation with my parents and aunt and uncle."

"About what?"

"Well, some of this depends on you—the last thing I want to do is rush you or pressure you. But if you still want to move to Durango, then I'd love to move with you…as your husband."

Hands flattened against his chest, she leaned back and raised an eyebrow. "My husband? Are you proposing?"

He chuckled. "I guess I am in a messed up kind of way."

She laughed and threw her arms around him. "It's not messed up at all."

Still holding on to her, Bear moved off the swing and knelt on the porch floor. "Piper Healy, I've loved you for more than fifteen years, even when you weren't mine. I promise to spend the rest of my days showing you just how much if you'd do the honor of becoming my wife."

With tears trailing down her cheeks, Piper's hand flew to her mouth as she nodded. "Yes, of course. But what if I don't move to Durango?"

"Well, I still want to marry you, but you may need to clear a drawer or two for me at your apartment."

"What about your cabin?"

Bear rubbed the back of his neck. "Well, the thing is, I'd like to use this property for something else. I'd like to work with Eugene and learn more about beekeeping. I have a nice chunk of land, and I'd like to add more yurts to establish the Ryland Healy Redemption Ranch and help cowboys with brain injuries find purpose again. I couldn't save Ry, but maybe we can prevent more families from going through what you and Avery did."

Piper covered her face with her hands and pressed her forehead against his shoulder. Her tiny body shook as sobs overcame her.

He wrapped his arms around her. "Hey, hey, if it's a bad idea, I won't do it. I promise. I don't want to do anything that upsets you."

Shaking her head, Piper pulled away and

dried her eyes with her fingers. "No, it's not that at all. Just the opposite. I think it's a beautiful idea. And I think it will honor Ry very well."

"This cabin could be used as the main house for whomever we get to oversee the program."

She cocked her head. "What if it's us?"

"What about Durango?"

"While I want Avery to have the very best education, perhaps I was the one doing the running. Avery gets upset every time we talk about it. I can talk with Everly and work with her school for satellite programs or some other form of enrichment to help with her educational needs. I think she'd thrive here, especially being around horses and knowing she was a part of her daddy's legacy in some way."

"After we're married, how would you feel about me adopting her?"

"I want to leave that decision up to her, but I have a feeling she will say yes. I will request, if you don't mind, that her last name be hyphenated, Healy-Stone, so she always has a part of Ry with her."

"I'm not trying to replace him. I just want her to know she's loved just as much as any other children we may have."

"Other children?" Her eyes widened.

He tapped the tip of her nose. "How do you feel about that?"

"I think I love the idea, but let's get married first before we rush any future plans."

"Sounds good to me." He lowered his head and captured her lips. He drew back and looked at her. "Is tomorrow too soon?"

"Just a little."

He'd waited for years to hold her in his arms. He could be patient a little longer to share his last name. He'd spend the rest of his life showing how much he loved her and be the family she'd always needed.

Epilogue

If anyone else had asked her to plan a wedding in two months, Piper would've laughed at the ridiculous request. But after Bear's proposal, they decided they wanted to ring in the New Year as husband and wife. They'd waited long enough.

The Stones had rallied, quick to reassure her they'd make it work. And they had.

Maybe she was being a little absurd, but a midnight candlelight ceremony under the stars seemed so romantic. It had snowed earlier in the day but stopped, and now the moon shone from a clear sky. The temperatures hadn't improved much, but she was too excited to feel the cold.

While so many were preparing to ring in the New Year, she was about to marry the man she loved.

"Ready, my dear?" Dressed in a dark gray suit with a burgundy-and-silver-striped tie with a bee tie tack and a wool overcoat, Eugene offered her his elbow.

"More than ready, my friend." Wearing Lynetta's altered wedding gown and a gorgeous white faux-fur full-length cape, Piper tucked a gloved hand in Eugene's elbow. Tightening her hold on her bouquet of burgundy, white and silver, she pressed a kiss to his shaven cheek. "Thank you, Eugene, for everything."

"Now don't get me all misty-eyed before I deliver you to your man. You know how much I care for you and your little one."

She rested her head against his shoulder, careful not to mess her curls, and nodded. "I do. And I'm so grateful."

He covered her hand with his and squeezed. "Let's get you married."

The instrumental music changed as Lynetta, her matron of honor and looking gorgeous in a floor-length burgundy lace gown, preceded her down the steps of Eugene's deck. She walked through the snow on a silver path lined with luminaries. Avery followed behind in her burgundy dress and cape that matched Piper's and scattered white rose petals on the silver aisle runner. The wind picked up and swirled them around her feet, which caused her daughter to giggle.

They reached Eugene's gazebo wrapped in tiny lights. Bear's family along with their closest friends held battery-powered candles as they gathered around the wooden structure, trying to stay warm.

The throaty notes of Etta James's "At Last" began playing, signaling Piper's cue to move toward her future husband.

Her love had come along, and Piper couldn't be more excited. Her eyes tangled with Bear's, allowing the glow of his wide smile to keep her warm and draw her to him.

Dressed in a gray suit, silver tie and his dress cowboy hat, and standing next to Wyatt, Bear stepped forward and offered his arm.

Eugene kissed her cheek and whispered, "He's a good man. I wish you two a blessed lifetime of happiness."

Tears welled in her eyes and she smiled through the sheen as she mouthed, "Thank you."

As she took Bear's arm, he leaned close, his mouth grazing her ear. "You look incredible."

She moved with him in front of their pastor. As she listened to the man's words about love, recited her vows and removed her glove to accept the ring he offered, she had no doubts about the choice she'd made. She was too enamored by the man promising to love her for the rest of his life.

A promise she'd hold him to.

As their pastor invited Bear to kiss his bride, his eyes shimmered in the candlelight. He stroked her cheek. "I love you, Mrs. Stone."

Her hand slid around his neck. "I love you, too, Mr. Stone."

As his lips found hers, their family and friends clapped and cheered.

"Three…two…one… Happy New Year!" Wyatt and Cole echoed behind them.

Bear brushed his lips to hers again. Then he pulled her into the warmth of his embrace—her favorite place. "Happy New Year, my love."

Moments later, as fresh snow fluttered over them, they hurried inside Eugene's gorgeous home, where Lynetta and Pete had prepared the perfect midnight wedding supper.

Too excited to eat, Piper mingled and laughed with their friends and family, Bear never more than an arm's reach away.

They made their way into the living room and snuggled close on Eugene's couch in front of the fireplace while the rest of the family cleared the tables. She sighed. "What a perfect night."

He kissed the top of her head. "It's going to be a perfect year—no matter what happens—because we'll spend it together."

Deacon, holding on to Nora's hand, moved in front of the fireplace. He clinked a knife against his glass as their family and friends moved into the room. "If I could have your attention, Nora and I have something we'd like to share."

Holding on to Bear's hand, Piper turned her attention to her new in-laws.

Deacon cleared his throat. "Piper, as a mother, you understand wanting only the best for your child. We feel the same way, and we are thrilled to welcome you into our family. You are the best for our son, and we couldn't be prouder of either of you."

Tears misted her eyes once again, but she forced them back as she smiled at the couple she now called Mom and Dad. She glanced at Bear, who ran a thumb under his eyes. "Thank you for accepting Avery and me into your family."

"You're one of us now, and that's why we would like the two of you to have this." Deacon reached inside his suit jacket pocket and pulled out an envelope. He handed it to Bear.

Frowning, Bear took it. "What's this?"

"It's the money you paid for the land you purchased to build your cabin. We put the check in the bank, knowing we wanted the land to be your inheritance someday. But you were stubborn and insisted on buying it. We are giving it to you as a wedding gift so you can invest it in the Ryland Healy Redemption Ranch. Since you're moving Piper and Avery into the cabin after your honeymoon, and Eugene keeps you so busy training you about beekeeping, we felt now was the best time to share it with you."

This time, Piper didn't bother trying to hold back the tears and allowed them to slide down her cheeks. She bit her lips to stifle the sob in her chest but to no avail.

The Stones' generosity—beginning with their son—overwhelmed her.

"Dad, I can't take this. What about the ranch? This money could be used to keep us in the black."

"Don't you worry about the ranch. God's got us and will see us through any storm."

"Amen to that." Bear stood and wrapped his parents in a hug. Then he reached for Piper. Wiping her eyes, she walked into their open arms, feeling complete for the first time in years.

She had a beautiful daughter, an incredible husband and a loving family to claim as her own. Their unconditional love proved she didn't have to be perfect. They accepted her as she was. And she couldn't be more grateful.

Eugene had been right—Bear's story didn't end with his mistakes. And neither did hers. God wasn't finished with either of them yet.

In fact, their story was just beginning with celebrating the New Year as husband and wife.

By surrendering their shame and fears, their tests became their testimonies as God redeemed the cowboy…and his bride.

* * * * *

Dear Reader,

Have you ever felt like you were defined by your past mistakes? Or maybe you feel as if love is conditional—based on performance or achievements, and taken away when you don't measure up?

Those are the lies Bear and Piper believed as they walked through life. Thankfully, they were able to accept the Truth. We serve a loving God, Who doesn't keep track of our mistakes. He loves us unconditionally. And His gift of grace is ours for the choosing.

I really enjoyed writing Bear and Piper's story, but it was one of the hardest books I've had to write. I had to actively seek Him to help my family through a crisis and to help me write this book. He showed up. The words flowed when I needed them to and I was able to meet my deadline. My heart rejoiced, knowing I could trust God to be there for me.

Perhaps, like Piper, you've been trying to go it alone for quite some time. Are you willing to lean into God's promises and allow Him to be your strength and shield? He hears your prayers and longs to help you bear anything life throws your way. It takes courage to trust Him and receive His redeeming grace.

Thank you for reading Bear and Piper's story. I hope you're eager to read about the rest of the Stone siblings as they walk through their own challenges.

I love hearing from my readers. Feel free to email me at lisa@lisajordanbooks.com. Visit my website at lisajordanbooks.com and sign up for my newsletter so you can be the first to learn about new book news.

Embrace His grace,
Lisa Jordan

Get 3 FREE REWARDS!

We'll send you 2 FREE Books plus a FREE Mystery Gift.

FREE
Value Over
$20

Both the **Love Inspired®** and **Love Inspired® Suspense** series feature compelling novels filled with inspirational romance, faith, forgiveness and hope.

YES! Please send me 2 FREE novels from the Love Inspired or Love Inspired Suspense series and my FREE gift (gift is worth about $10 retail). After receiving them, if I don't wish to receive any more books, I can return the shipping statement marked "cancel." If I don't cancel, I will receive 6 brand-new Love Inspired Larger-Print books or Love Inspired Suspense Larger-Print books every month and be billed just $6.49 each in the U.S. or $6.74 each in Canada. That is a savings of at least 16% off the cover price. It's quite a bargain! Shipping and handling is just 50¢ per book in the U.S. and $1.25 per book in Canada.* I understand that accepting the 2 free books and gift places me under no obligation to buy anything. I can always return a shipment and cancel at any time by calling the number below. The free books and gift are mine to keep no matter what I decide.

Choose one: ☐ **Love Inspired**   ☐ **Love Inspired**   ☐ **Or Try Both!**
              Larger-Print   **Suspense**   (122/322 & 107/307
              (122/322 BPA GRPA)   **Larger-Print**   BPA GRRP)
                                            (107/307 BPA GRPA)

Name (please print)

Address   Apt. #

City   State/Province   Zip/Postal Code

Email: Please check this box ☐ if you would like to receive newsletters and promotional emails from Harlequin Enterprises ULC and its affiliates. You can unsubscribe anytime.

Mail to the **Harlequin Reader Service:**
IN U.S.A.: P.O. Box 1341, Buffalo, NY 14240-8531
IN CANADA: P.O. Box 603, Fort Erie, Ontario L2A 5X3

Want to try 2 free books from another series! Call 1-800-873-8635 or visit www.ReaderService.com.

*Terms and prices subject to change without notice. Prices do not include sales taxes, which will be charged (if applicable) based on your state or country of residence. Canadian residents will be charged applicable taxes. Offer not valid in Quebec. This offer is limited to one order per household. Books received may not be as shown. Not valid for current subscribers to the Love Inspired or Love Inspired Suspense series. All orders subject to approval. Credit or debit balances in a customer's account(s) may be offset by any other outstanding balance owed by or to the customer. Please allow 4 to 6 weeks for delivery. Offer available while quantities last.

Your Privacy—Your information is being collected by Harlequin Enterprises ULC, operating as Harlequin Reader Service. For a complete summary of the information we collect, how we use this information and to whom it is disclosed, please visit our privacy notice located at corporate.harlequin.com/privacy-notice. From time to time we may also exchange your personal information with reputable third parties. If you wish to opt out of this sharing of your personal information, please visit readerservice.com/consumerchoice or call 1-800-873-8635. **Notice to California Residents**—Under California law, you have specific rights to control and access your data. For more information on these rights and how to exercise them, visit corporate.harlequin.com/california-privacy.

LIRLIS23

Get 3 FREE REWARDS!

We'll send you 2 FREE Books plus a FREE Mystery Gift.

FREE Value Over $20

Both the **Harlequin® Special Edition** and **Harlequin® Heartwarming™** series feature compelling novels filled with stories of love and strength where the bonds of friendship, family and community unite.

YES! Please send me 2 FREE novels from the Harlequin Special Edition or Harlequin Heartwarming series and my FREE Gift (gift is worth about $10 retail). After receiving them, if I don't wish to receive any more books, I can return the shipping statement marked "cancel." If I don't cancel, I will receive 6 brand-new Harlequin Special Edition books every month and be billed just $5.49 each in the U.S. or $6.24 each in Canada, a savings of at least 12% off the cover price, or 4 brand-new Harlequin Heartwarming Larger-Print books every month and be billed just $6.24 each in the U.S. or $6.74 each in Canada, a savings of at least 19% off the cover price. It's quite a bargain! Shipping and handling is just 50¢ per book in the U.S. and $1.25 per book in Canada.* I understand that accepting the 2 free books and gift places me under no obligation to buy anything. I can always return a shipment and cancel at any time by calling the number below. The free books and gift are mine to keep no matter what I decide.

Choose one: ☐ **Harlequin Special Edition** (235/335 BPA GRMK)   ☐ **Harlequin Heartwarming Larger-Print** (161/361 BPA GRMK)   ☐ **Or Try Both!** (235/335 & 161/361 BPA GRPZ)

Name (please print)

Address   Apt. #

City   State/Province   Zip/Postal Code

Email: Please check this box ☐ if you would like to receive newsletters and promotional emails from Harlequin Enterprises ULC and its affiliates. You can unsubscribe anytime.

Mail to the Harlequin Reader Service:
IN U.S.A.: P.O. Box 1341, Buffalo, NY 14240-8531
IN CANADA: P.O. Box 603, Fort Erie, Ontario L2A 5X3

Want to try 2 free books from another series! Call 1-800-873-8635 or visit www.ReaderService.com.